The Eternity Symbiote

Cedar Sanderson

Other Titles by Author

Short Stories and Novellas

Voyageur's Cap (Published by Naked Reader Press) - Space Pirates and the return of the Hudson's Bay Company.

Memories of the Abyss - She may be crazy, but she knows her only friend was murdered.

Stargazer - Science fiction short story of a mother's love.

The Twisted Breath of God - A story of second contact with aliens.

Little Red-Hood and the Wolf-Man - Who's afraid of the big bad wolf? Not little Red with her shotgun!

Dwarf's Dryad - Who rescues whom from the Witch and her rapunzel?

Plant Life - Exploration of a new planet and first contact.

Snow Angel - A mother's love can defy any power, even that of angels.

Milkweed - Mythic Delirium #4

Novels

Pixie Noir - Book one in the Pixie for Hire series.

Trickster Noir - Book two of Pixie for Hire, to be released May 2014

Vulcan's Kittens - A novel of mythological beings and their children.

Dedicated to the Baen Barflies, who inspired me to start writing this story, and ultimately, to publish it.

Table of Contents

Meeting by Misadventure

Gabrielle McGregor ran her fingers through her hair, stretching upwards onto her toes, and yawned. It had been a long flight, with only the prospect of another long one ahead of her. A quiet one, too. She had never seen her charter passengers before, and they had not introduced themselves when they arrived at the little airport she worked out of. The tiny Tok airport was the last jumping-off point for much of the bush country in Alaska, and she was used to charters for Fairbanks or Anchorage, but this was a unusual one for her - all the way out into the Forty-Mile area, to a small lake the size of a pocket-handkerchief. The passengers were unusual too - the military ordinarily found it cheaper to fly their own people to out-of the-way places in the Alaskan wilderness than to charter a bush pilot.

Only minutes before she had landed neatly on her pontoons and helped her passengers out. Now she stood on the rickety dock while her two passengers made their way to the shore and argued about something. Well, when they made up their minds she'd help them unload, and then head for town. The deal was, she would drop off, and then when their three days were up, they would be picked up. Probably not by her, as there were three other pilots who also worked for the air ferry service, and that was fine with her. She was not a gregarious woman, but it was unnerving to fly for four hours and not have one of them say a word. One had slept, mostly, while the other had pulled out a PDA and tapped away at it the whole trip.

She was just contemplating climbing back into the plane for a quick nap when one of the men came down the dock to her.

"Er, sorry about that. But we thought we had come to the wrong lake."

"Oh?" she asked cooly, feeling her navigational skills slighted.

"Oh, no, you got us where we wanted to be," he assured her hastily. "But there was supposed to be someone here waiting for us."

That confused her. How would this person have gotten out here? As far as she knew, no-one had gotten a flight out here in a very long time. Shrugging, she offered to help with their luggage.

"Thank you, ma'am. I do appreciate this," he took the first bags from her - mostly camping gear, she noted - and set them on the dock.

He was not a prepossessing man, average height and build, which meant she stood nose-to-nose with him, as she was tall for a woman. Brown hair, and pale brown eyes, she observed now. His partner, still staring out into the wood, no doubt hoping for the arrival of their missing person, was shorter, and stocky, with close-cut black hair that he had run his fingers through, and which now stood on end. They looked capable enough, she thought, running her eyes over the camping gear they had brought, which was not new. She didn't think she needed to worry about leaving them on their own out here.

"The bears out here aren't shy," she did finally warn. "They probably haven't seen a person, and likely they'll just hightail it if they see you, but they just might get curious and decide to poke around."

He smiled. "Thank you. We hopefully will not be here long."

Her curiosity piqued, she asked, "Aren't you camping?"

"Only if necessary. Really, we're just here to pick something up. Our missing member of the team was to have

located it, and we were to merely help
him retrieve it."

"And what would that be? We don't fly
live animals, and it is out of season for
most everything." Her steely eyes warned
him that she, personally, did not care to
look the other way if they were poaching.

"No, no, nothing like that." He
looked startled. "No, we are trying to
find a meteor."

She raised her eyebrows. "Isn't that
unlikely, in all this?" she gestured
around them at the vast, empty
wilderness.

"Well," he hefted up two of the bags
and set off toward shore with her
following. "It was a very unusual
meteor."

She could tell he was hedging, but at
least he was talking, and her overactive
curiosity bump wanted scratching. "So,
what is it that you do?"

"Well, they are with NASA, I am a
consultant." He dropped the bags on the
ground as they stepped off the dock, and
when she followed suit, stuck out his
hand to be shaken. "Paul Monroe is my
name - er, there is a doctorate involved,
but I don't use it. Confusing you know,"
his eyes twinkled at her.

She laughed, a singular, low laugh
that she knew men loved to hear, and
shook hands.

"Gabrielle McGregor, nice to meet you."

She turned to see the other man striding back out of the woods, looking frustrated.

"I can't think where he is." The shorter man growled at Paul without ceremony.

"Major Dexter Guptill, meet Ms. McGregor." said Paul calmly.

The man glared at Paul, then reluctantly shook her hand. "Thank you for the ride," he said brusquely. "We will be fine from here." he finished, dismissing her.

"All right then." she inclined her head gracefully. "When you call, someone will be back to get you."

She was folding herself into the plane when she heard a shout. Looking out the still-open door, she saw Paul racing up the dock, waving his hand.

"Wait!" he called.

She stepped back onto the dock.

Puffing slightly, he grinned. "No need to call - he's here and with the rock!"

She turned to see Major Guptill and another man bent over a bundle wrapped in olive green cloth - parachute silk, if she guessed correctly. She shrugged. They were paying, she was just their ride.

"Are we headed back to town, then?"

He nodded.

"All right, grab your bags."

Paul trotted back down the dock with her, saying breathlessly, "I'm sorry he was rude. They have some idea this needed to be a secret." He snorted. "I could have told them there was no need. I mean, I love to get a look at meteors when I can, but we already know what most of them are composed of. The probability of something previously unknown coming in is so small as to be vanishing. I have no idea why they wanted me along for this, but it pays well, and was definitely a break from the daily grind, so here I am!"

She helped him load the bags in, and then climbed back in herself and began to run her checklist. The rude major had not bothered her, and the flirtatious consultant was charming enough. She just wanted to get home.

She was absorbed in her task and did not look up for the two men as they walked down the dock. She could hear them settling their burden in the back and realized with slight annoyance that one of them meant to sit beside her. She looked up and her eyes widened. She emitted a slight squeak of surprise, and the tall man sliding into the seat next to her grinned and said,

"I love that sound, Gabi! Oh, God, such an undignified noise to make and at such a time!"

Quickly, she recovered herself and replied acerbically, "Anyone would make a noise if they looked up into that mug looming over them!"

Lieutenant Colonel Jedediah McGregor - the penultimate tall, dark, and handsome man - buckled himself in and leaned over to peck her on the cheek. "How are you, cherie?"

Paul leaned forward, fascinated at their by-play. "Do you two - ah - know one another?"

Jed turned his head, raising one dark eyebrow and laughing, as Gabi taxied out into the lake.

"Why, Paul, she's my wife."

The other man blinked in surprise. "Er, oh."

Once they were airborne, Jed spoke softly to Gabi. "Sorry I didn't give you a call while I was in town, but I needed to get this little job done."

"So what is it about a meteor that requires a Ranger and a NASA muckety-muck, not to mention a 'consultant', to retrieve?"

"Oho, someone told you, eh?"

He looked back at Paul, who blushed slightly. "All I said was that it was an unusual meteor."

Gabi raised her eyebrow. "I don't believe that for a minute. Why would they have hauled you out of mothballs to hunt down a rock in the bush? I don't expect you to tell me, though, I understand need-to-know."

"Why not?" he shrugged. "A UFO crashed out there."

She looked hard at him, banking absent-mindedly into her heading for Tok. He met her gaze seriously, his mouth hard. She saw that he believed it, and it unsettled him. She looked at him for a moment, drinking in the familiar features - The aquiline nose, the gentle lips, the mobile eyebrows - all of which she knew by heart, had learned by braille in their dark bedroom, as well as in the light across the breakfast table. His dark hair was graying rapidly, she noted with a pang, but his lean body must be in the same fighting fit shape it had always been, if he were still going out on remote missions. She looked at her instruments and then out the windshield. The changeless, featureless forest spread out below them. It was dotted here and there with lakes, or stretches of muskeg where the permafrost was so close to the surface it stunted the spruce growing on it until they were not much taller than a man. On this inhospitable footing the trees were spaced widely, with dwarf birch, alders, willows, and blueberries making a tangled mat of vegetation between them.

She saw Jed out of the corner of her eye, leaning his head back and closing his eyes. Her heart softened at his obvious weariness, and she thought about their relationship. They had married almost eight years before, when they were both still in the military, and they were almost immediately stationed across the world from one another. When they did end up in the same place, she felt like she did not know him, and she chose not to reenlist, but Jed was not ready to leave the Service.

They had argued, she wanting him close, he feeling guilty for not being near, but wanting to live his life. She had felt confined, living on base, and felt like she had to become something she was not, to further his career. This was worsened by her problems at work. Finally she could no longer bear it, and she fled. She had stormed out of their home, where they had spent only one year out of the two they had spent together, and had flown to Alaska. Once there, she deeply regretted running from him, but her pride would not allow her to return to him. She had written him, letting him know where she was, and that she planned to stay. As the years passed, she found herself lonely. He had visited her, letting her know that he would not pressure her into a life that would make her unhappy. He told her that he only wanted her happy, and that she would always be his wife, whenever she wanted to see him, or perhaps even live with him again. They had met a few times, after that, for a week or two. Like little honeymoons, but always she returned to Alaska, and always he sat with his head in his hands after she was gone and wondered how many more times he could withstand this heart wrenching, and if she would ever consent to be his again.

It had been six months since the last time they had met, in Seattle. They had barely gotten into the hotel room before tearing one another's clothes off, and they each knew, falling in to bed together, that the other was still faithful to them. At the end of their long weekend together, Gabi had woken up before he had, and leaned on her elbow, watching him sleep. He looked so young, at rest, and her heart smote her, for she guessed at his pain every time she left. But she remembered the past, and her unhappiness, and steeled herself to leave him yet again.

At the airport he had held her for a long time, gently kissing her eyes, face, and lips. Finally he had cradled her in his arms for a moment, and she saw tears in his eyes.

"Gabi," he began, huskily "I can't do this anymore. I can't say goodbye to you anymore. I thought I could - could just let you be free. But I need you." he put a finger on her lips, stopping her reply.

"I'm not asking you to do anything. Just telling you that the next time I need you to come to me. I..." his voice broke, and he stopped, tears on his cheeks now. She looked mutely up at him, dumb in the face of his emotion.

They heard her flight called. Her dropped his arms, freeing her. She stood still for a minute, her heart in her throat. Then she whispered, "I'm afraid."

They had another hour to go. Gabi stretched in her seat, flexing stiff neck and shoulders. Paul and the major were both asleep, she saw, and Jed was silently watching her.

He smiled when he met her eyes and murmured "ma cherie, j'taime beaucoup."

"J'taime aussi," she replied, and her heart was in her eyes.

He caught his breath and sat up. "Gabi..."

She shook her head, looking back at her sleeping passengers.

"So are you going home after you deliver your package?" she asked.

A flame leaped up in his eyes, hope renewed. "Yes."

"Mind company? I'll need a couple of weeks to wrap it up here, but I've just finished training my replacement..."

He laughed, a low, joyful sound.

"Gabi." his voice was almost a growl, caressing, and she shivered with the emotion. "Girl..." he was reaching out

his hand to her when there was a bang,
and her vision went black.

Crash Landings

Jed ducked, instinctively, as the glass of the windshield imploded, along with ten pounds of dead bird. Gasping, he looked up to see his wife, slumped over the yoke of the plane. Already it was diving, yawing erratically. He reached over and pushed her back and pulled up on the yoke with his free hand. The plane started to level out, then pitched forward as the pontoons caught the tip of an unusually tall spruce. He fought with the controls, leaning all the way across the little cockpit and holding his wife up with his elbow, more or less. The Paul's arm came around the seat and held Gabi's shoulder.

'Thanks," Jed growled, not taking his eyes off the trees rushing by just below them. Abruptly they thinned and he saw another small lake ahead. "I'm going to try and land."

Gabi stirred and reached out for the controls.

"Got - got it," she whispered.

She slowed them as much as she could and at an angle, they approached the lake. With the first hard bounce, the air in the cockpit filled with a gray dust. Gabi sneezed, and the plane slewed and plowed into the water, hard. Then it stopped, halfway over, and slowly righted, much to its sneezing passengers' relief.

Jed opened his door, and the dust slowly dissipated. Gabi, coughing and moaning, bent over the yoke again. Jed touched her hair, and brought away bloody fingertips.

"Gabi..." he began, but then Paul broke in, an edge to his voice.

"Captain McGregor, you need to look at Major Guptill."

Jed turned around, to see the Major hanging slackly against his restraints, head down. Paul was feeling for a pulse, then he shook his head.

"He's gone," he announced grimly.

"What happened?" Gabi whispered.

"A bird hit us."

Jed moved the dead man's arm and winced as the man's head rolled to one side and revealed the long shard of glass impaling his neck. "It must have gone right into the artery," he murmured. "Paul, are you all right?"

"Um, no. I seem to have a hole in my thigh, myself," he grimaced. "Think you could take a look?"

Later, after Jed had bandaged Paul's thigh and had swum in the gaspingly cold water to tow the plane to shore, and had a small fire built to dry off by and make Gabi and Paul comfortable, he tried to radio for assistance. To his dismay, the radio was inoperative. He couldn't figure out quite what had gone wrong, but he guessed that one of the jolts the equipment had undergone that day had finished it off. Cursing under his breath, he returned to where Paul sat and Gabi lay, her head pillowed on his field jacket.

Her face was drawn with pain, but she was bravely trying to stay awake, as they knew she must have a concussion at least. "Jed, what was that dust?"

He shook his head, sitting next to her and taking her hand.

Paul answered "I think it was inside the 'meteor'. Which, by the way, looks like no meteor I ever saw." He held it out . It was a small box, about the size of a basketball. It was hinged at the top, and the upper third of it was off, and the hinge broken. It was still filled with what remained of the gray dust. The outside of it was metallic, but iridescent, and the inside of it was filled with white crystals, which were audibly shattering as they looked, and steaming gently.

"Like some strange geode." Gabi commented.

"Yeah." agreed their resident geologist, taking it back and bending his head over it. He touched one of them gingerly, and winced. "Ouch! it burnt me!"

He stuck the injured finger in his mouth, reflexively, then pulled it out with an odd expression on his face. "No, it froze me."

Gabi tried to sit up, urgently "Let me see th..."

She turned slightly green and lay back down, hastily.

Jed stretched. "How long until we can expect a rescue?"

"About seventy-two hours until the first overflight, generally. You don't want to go whacking through these woods, trust me."

Jed grimaced in agreement. "I had a devil of a time getting to the rendezvous point through all that. I don't want to carry you through the woods, however romantic a notion it is, Gabi."

She closed her eyes for a moment and he realized how much pain she was in. Her face was drawn and gray with it. "Gabi? don't fall asleep on me," he commanded gently.

She opened her eyes again. "Just resting. I am thirsty, though. Could you get me one of the jugs out of the plane?"

Jed brought back one of the two gallon jugs and a coffee mug he had rinsed out in the lake. He supported her head and shoulders while she took a drink of water, and then helped her get comfortable.

"I want to see how bad it is." He touched her scalp gently, palpating the injured area. Paul looked worriedly on from the other side of the fire, his leg stretched out stiffly.

Jed slid his hands down to hold her cheeks. "Gabi, your skull is fractured. Not depressed, but definitely not intact, either."

She nodded slightly. "Well, let's hope it doesn't swell too much." She tried to say lightly, but it did not come over well. Both men could see the fear on her face. She tried to get their attention off herself. "Paul, how is your leg?"

"Okay. It really smarts, but it stopped bleeding. I don't think it'll even need stitches."

Gabi smiled, and yawned. "So how are we going to keep me awake?"

Jed grinned down at her, his heart heavy at her pain. He was forcing himself to be cheerful. He had gotten angry too many times in the past at her pain. He could not help it. When something was wrong, he wanted to fix it, and he had never reacted well when he could only sit and do nothing about it. But tonight he was determined to keep her spirits - all of their spirits - up until help came. Just as so many time in the past, he was in command, and morale was his responsibility.

"How about campfire songs?"

Gabi groaned and rolled her eyes. Paul laughed and sang "I'm having a wonderful time but I'd rather be whistling in the dark..."

Gabi giggled. "Oh great, if we're going down that road, how about ghost stories?"

"How about Jed tells us what's really going on with the UFO?" Paul suggested

Jed made a face at him, appreciating his willingness to play along with the effort to lift the gloomy mood that had hung over them. "Just so you stop with the 'they might be giants' songs. That one always sticks in my mind for days."

"Well, let's see, where do I begin? I don't know all of the story, mind. Colonel Matthewson called me in because he knows me, trusts me, and knows I have an open mind. He told me that we had been contacted by aliens, and that after a lot of discussion, it was finally decided that we would host them here in the US of A for their first landing on Earth. A small landing ship headed in, carrying an ambassador and his retinue, as I understand it, but something went wrong and they crashed here in Alaska. They had come in over the pole to reduce the odds of being seen. I guess the powers that be are still trying to figure out how to break this to the general public."

"Wow." Paul interrupted, looking up at the darkening sky. The first stars were beginning to come out. "There really is someone out there, then."

"Yes, and I have seen them. They wanted us to find the ship and mark it so they can come and get their casualties. They were afraid that searching for it themselves would attract to much attention, and they couldn't get into a close enough earth orbit to find it with their scanners without the same problem. So the Colonel called on me. After I got through pointing out that I was a little old for this kind of thing, he told me he wanted someone with a little more experience and intelligence than your average grunt."

Jed looked down at Gabi, who was struggling to keep her eyes open. "Hey, am I boring you?"

"No, no, this is fascinating," she tried to smile.

"OK. So the Army shipped me off to Eilson, and a Blackhawk dropped me at the crash site after we found it. Finding it took about a week. I wanted to come down and see you, Gabi, but they were keeping pretty tight tabs on me. Anyway, we had instructions from the aliens not to allow anyone but me too close to the wreck, so I went in alone and put a beacon on it for them, made to their specs. I turned it on, and then took a good look around."

"What do they look like?"

"I don't want to talk about it. They'd been dead a week, and the animals had been at them. All I know is that they look a lot more like a man than made me happy. Anyway, I had been told to look for that thing." He nodded at the box lying next to Paul, rewrapped in a neat package of parachute silk.

"What is it?" Gabi asked faintly.

"They told us it is a gift to humanity. I have no friggin' idea what it really is. I'm not to sure about the gift part, with seven of them dead and one of ours."

Paul flinched at the reminder of the dead man, still in the plane.

"Should... should we take the major out of the plane?" he asked tentatively.

"No, I think the officials will want to satisfy themselves that he really did die in the accident. Besides, we probably couldn't move him by now. Oh, rat's ass. I forgot to get the survival kit out. Are you hungry?"

"No, I feel really nauseated," replied Gabi, to whom he had addressed the question. "Paul?"

"Yeah, I'm hungry." he admitted reluctantly. "How can you be so... so... calm about Major Guptill?"

Jed gave him a twisted smile, rueful. "I've seen a lot of dead bodies, and one thing I know about them. They are harmless. The person that used to be in there is gone. The thing that is left behind is so much cold clay and there isn't a thing I can do about it."

He got up and headed for the plane. He carried a red flashlight to guide him to the water's edge, careful over the rough ground. The white of the fuselage glimmered in the starlight. The moon was just rising. He stopped and looked up into the sky, into the brilliance of the stars. Nowhere else on earth could you see the sky quite like here, he thought. The air was absolutely clear, and the light of the stars was illuminating. He raised his fist and growled at the unseen craft far above.

"She dies, and I'm coming to get you, bastards."

On the way back, pack in hand, he could see the glimmer of the fire and hear their voices. Paul was saying "Yeah, Mom is a really nice lady. More than makes up for Dad's preoccupation with his work. What about your family?"

Gabi glanced up at Jed, who smiled at her and dropped down by the fire. He dug in the pack and handed Paul two MRE's. "Your choice of Tuna and Noodles, or Beef Stew."

"Oh, gross! Not the tuna, Jed!" Gabi protested. "Poor guy."

"Well, I guess that means I should choose the beef," Paul handed the other one back to Jed with a lopsided grin.

He tore it open and got it ready to heat in a canteen cup. "You were telling him about your family, Gabi?"

"Hmmm... well, I have a lot of family here in Alaska. I live with my Dad and and uncle, actually. They were batching it for years, after my Mom died, and it has taken them some adjusting to get used to having a woman around the house again. You know, little things like curtains, hot meals at home... The Northstar called me and complained that I had lost them two of their best customers. I compromised with them and only cook one meal a day for the guys, now. My cousins live out in the bush. They guide cheechakos out for big game. Some of them are decent enough, but..."

She trailed off, staring into space. Jed looked hard at her, feeling worried. It was unlike her to ramble or get confused. He cleared his throat. "How about the story of the blue and yellow wolves?"

"Huh? oh, all right..." she thought for a moment, then began "well, my second cousin went to college in the Southeast, and studied Forestry. S... no, wait, it was Uncle Jim... I think." she trailed off with puckered brow, staring into space as if expecting the story to pop into sight in midair.

To hide his concern, Jed started to get up to get some more wood. There was plenty of dry, dead branches on the trees, but being black spruce, they were like twigs and good only for kindling. He thought he had seen a dead tree earlier, though. As he tried to stand, he felt the sweat pop out on his forehead, and his head spun. He sat back down heavily and put his head between his knees, sucking in deep breaths of the chilly air. He looked up at Paul when his head cleared, and saw that he, too, was looking rather pale.

"You all right?"

"No... Look!" and he pointed at Gabi, who was having a convulsion.

"Oh, sh..." Jed leapt to her side, trying to ignore his rising gorge. He held her firmly, trying to keep her from rolling into the fire. When it had passed, her eyes were closed and her face bathed in sweat. Jed was dimly aware that Paul had rolled over and gotten to his hands and knees and was puking his guts up.

"Oh, shit," he got out. Then he, too, lost his dinner.

He managed not to get any on Gabi, and afterwards knelt next to her, feeling weaker than he ever had before. He felt

like he was burning up, too. Her eyes
were still closed, and he started to
shake her, then stopped, thinking of her
head injury. He tried slapping her cheeks
gently, then tickling the palms of her
hands, something he had done years ago to
wake her up. She didn't stir.

"Jed?" Paul asked hoarsely.

"Can you get me the flashlight?"

"Yeah... I'll try."

A minute later he crawled over with
it, evidently afraid to try to stand up.
Jed felt him put it into his hand. he
couldn't take his eyes off of his wife's
still face. He twisted off the red filter
and lifted her eyelid to shine it into
her eye. Her pupil stayed dilated.

"Oh, shit." he said again, sagging
back onto his heels.

"What? What's wrong?"

"She's in a coma."

Regeneration

Both Jed and Paul vomited several
times in the night, dry heaves after all
else had come up. Paul managed to sleep
finally, shortly before dawn. Jed lay
next to Gabi all that night, staring into
the darkness, worrying. He had been
pushing long and hard, though, and he
fell asleep just as the first light
touched the mountains. He slept deeply
and dreamlessly. When he woke, it was
midday. He blinked up at the trees
overhead, feeling rather bleary and
tasting such a foul mouth that he almost
gagged on it. He was starving, and
thirsty, he realized. He sat up and
checked on Gabi.

She was the same as she had been.
Still, so still. His heart skipped a
beat, and he kissed her forehead. She
felt normal. The fever of the night
before had gone. He sighed, and looked
over to see Paul lying on his side,
peacefully asleep. Relaxed in sleep, he
looked very young, and Jed felt very old.
He pushed himself to his feet, surprised
first at how little soreness he felt, and
second at just how hungry he was. His
stomach felt hollow. He pulled and MRE
out of the pack and ate it without even
heating it. Feeling slightly better, he

stirred up the fire and put another one on to heat for Paul. As he started to smell it, Paul stirred.

"Oooh," he put a hand to his head. Then, "That smells great. I'm famished!"

Jed silently handed him the cup and heated another one for himself. Paul finished his and asked, "Any change?"

Jed shook his head. He didn't feel like talking this morning. He offered Paul a cup of water.

"Thanks. Don't fret so much. She'll be fine. She's tough."

"Yeah. How's your leg."

"I hadn't even thought about it yet." He threw back his sleeping bag and looked down, then back up at Jed, a bemused look on his face. Jed came around the fire to see.

There was no sign of the wound. Jed did not think that was possible. It had been quite deep - well into the muscle, with some imbedded glass. Paul pulled the bandage off, and the only thing that remained was a faint scar, and the blood on his trousers and the bandage. He shook the bandage, and a few pieces of glass fell out, glittering in the moss. He poked at his leg, hesitantly at first, then harder.

"It doesn't hurt," he marveled, breathless.

"Well, I'll be..." Jed sat down next to him, and they stared at the unbroken skin for a long moment. Then Paul stood up. He stood still for a moment, then took a few steps. Grinning now, he stood on one leg.

Behind them, they heard a noise. Jed spun around to see Gabi tossing in her sleep, whimpering. He rushed to her side and felt her forehead. Still normal. What was wrong. She mewled and rubbed her cheek against his hand, making smacking sounds with her lips. He felt Paul's presence next to he, staring, as he was at the unconscious woman and trying to decipher her behavior.

"Jed," Paul began hesitantly. "Maybe she's hungry."

"Yeah..." Jed turned to the kit and rummaged. Protein bars. yuch. "Can you get some water, please?"

"From the lake?" Paul protested.

"Yes!" Jed snapped. He started to break the bars up into the tiny aluminum pot she'd had in her kit. They were remote enough the water should be pure, and anyway, he planned to boil it.

Paul scrambled away with the empty canteen and returned in a minute, wet to the knees.

"thanks." Jed had built the fire up and now put the pot close with the cold mixture of water and protein bar chunks in it. Paul helped him prop Gabi up and they started to give her water. She drank greedily, eyes half open, but, as Paul commented solemnly 'no-one home'.

Finally the soup got warm, then boiled. Jed let it go for a minute or two, but then he couldn;t wait any longer. The smell made Gabi restless and he was afraid she would hurt herself with so much movement. Paul started another batch in the canteen cup as Jed fed Gabi the first pot. She ate without reaction, as she had drunk, but almost snapping at him when he didn't move fast enough.

They fed her four batches and were almost out of bars when she closed her eyes abruptly and fell asleep. Paul sat still with her head propped on his shoulder and stared at Jed, who was still holding a full spoon in his hand, ready to give her another bite.

"Man alive." He whispered. "What is going on?"

Jed shook his head, feeling the fatigue soak into his bones. It had been a long tie since he'd felt this tired. Like he could just lie down and sleep where he was. He ate the spoonful of soup absently. And hungry. He thought he'd been a teenager the last time he'd felt hunger pangs like this. He looked at Paul, who had settled Gabi back down, and noticed the dark circles under his eyes for the first time.

"Hungry?"

"Oh, God, yes," the young man sighed.

They ate the rest of the food between them. Jed thought they should save some, but he couldn't help it. The urge to fuel his body was more than he could resist, and it frightened him to lose control like this. Paul abruptly curled up on the moss and went to sleep. Jed had barely drawn a sleeping bag over him when he felt sleep roll over him like a fog and he fell...

He woke at dawn, alert and warm. It had been dusk when he'd collapsed, and he'd slept through the night next to what was left of the fire. He moved and felt the sleeping bag fall off him. Confused, he sat up, wondering whether Paul had woken before him. Across the lively fire in the dim light, he looked into Gabi's smiling eyes. Paul was lounging on the ground in his bag, grinning up at him.

Jed felt his heart racing. Dumfounded, he looked back and forth between the two of them.

"What... what is happening?" he finally managed.

Gabi touched her hair, encrusted with dried blood, and made a face. But her long fingers continued to massage her scalp, and she kept smiling. "Come feel!" she invited. "Wait..."

Jed held his breath.

"Let me wash my hair first," she continued with a wrinkled nose.

Both Jed and Paul roared with
laughter. After an instant, Gabi joined
them. They laughed for quite a while,
washing away the fears and tensions of
that long night. Finally, gasping for
breath, Gabi announced that she really
was going to go rinse her hair out.
When she had gone down to the marshy edge
of the lake, Paul asked, "Jed, do you
think we ought to look at Major Guptill?"

Jed looked at him in horror. "Maybe I
should." he said finally.

"Shall I come with you?"

"No."

Jed felt strangely nervous as he
approached the plane. He could see the
slumped figure through the window, but he
opened the door and reached up to take
his pulse, anyway. He was not sure
whether he was relieved or disappointed
at the cold, still flesh of the dead man.
He stared at him for a minute, knowing
that Gabi could easily have died the
night before, and knowing that whatever
had happened, it was not natural. He felt
the warmth of the sun on his back, and
turning away from the plane, saw his
surroundings with new eyes.

The lake they had landed on
encompassed no more than an acre in size,
but it shimmered in the sun like a jewel.
Lilypads dotted its surface, and the
thick, quiet forest pressed in around it.
The forest was what worried him. Hundreds

of miles of it, all the same, broken only occasionally by a lake or pond like this one. Even the quaking aspen stands were still covered in leaves, although they were turning golden and would fall soon. The only place a searcher from above could see those who were lost was out in the open - and there were virtually no open places out here. Jed knew the plane would be a dead giveaway to searchers for them, and he knew they needed to stick close to it.

Gabi came towards him, walking gingerly through the thick willow growth near the water. He waved, and walked to meet her, not wanting her to dwell on the body. When they met, he pulled her into his arms and held her for a long moment, feeling unusually emotional.

She leaned back to look at him. "My head is completely healed. So is Paul's leg. Any ideas why?"

He shook his head. "Let's get back to camp."

Back at their little camp, Paul was dug in the pack Jed had brought up from the plane. He looked up and grinned. "Hey, Jed, were you a boy scout? You're prepared for anything!"

He pointed at the array of food he had. "I thought I'd make a stew or something."

"Oh, you angel!" Gabi crowed. "I'm ravenous."

"I thought so." Jed said. "Have either of you noticed how hungry we all were this morning?"

Gabi nodded. "Yes. And thirsty."

"Gabi, is what happened possible?"

"what do you mean by possible? Obviously, it happened, unless all three of us are experiencing an unusually detailed and particularly pleasant mass hallucination. Is there any precedent for it? No."

She sighed and sat down, reaching for a packet of dried fruit and nuts. "I have no idea, frankly, what happened or how it happened. All I can say is that after the accident I had a fractured skull, and today I don't even have a scar. The only way I can prove I had an injury is an area of hair that has been cut off." She flipped her hair over to show them the ragged place.

Paul offered her a canteen cup. She looked in it and laughed. "Thank you! blueberries, mmm."

"There's bushes of 'em right over there," he indicated proudly.

"Damn." Jed swore.

"What?" Paul looked startled at this reaction to his discovery.

"Bears," Gabi interjected. "I have my gun, Jed." She showed him the forty-four in her shoulder holster. He cocked an eyebrow at it.

"Isn't that a lot of gun for you?"

"Yes, but anything less won't stop a big brownie. Dad makes me shoot fifty rounds every month with it."

"Yeah, well..." he looked around suspiciously, as if expecting a bear to step into view.

"We could move camp, but there are probably berries right around the lake. Let's just try to keep the noise level up. Most of them out here are shy. Not like the ones in town. Last summer Dad and Uncle Jim took out twenty-two black bears at the town dump."

Jed tossed a filter bottle of water to her. "Thanks. Like I was saying, I really wish I knew _how_ we healed so quickly. Normally," she addressed Paul, "the human body has to go through a number of steps, and a lot of time, to accomplish what we went through in a matter of hours. Jed, I have a sneaking suspicion that your 'gift to humanity' had something to do with this. I just wish I knew what it was.

"You mean, that dust healed us?"

Gabi wrinkled her nose in thought. "No, I can't think how it would have. What I think is that there is a lot more to that stuff than meets the eye. What I wouldn't give for a good microscope. Scanning Electron, preferably."

She sighed, a far-off look in her eyes. Jed snorted. "Never stand between a scientist and her subject." he advised Paul.

"A scientist? but I thought..."

She chuckled, not losing her thoughtful gaze into the distance. "Thought I was a simple bush pilot, didn't you?"

Jed answered "She is a brilliant epidemiologist, Infections diseases, not the namby-pamby health food style they raise now,. She used to be a real brain - long hair tied back in a bun, glasses, that horrible army green suit," he wiggled his eyebrows at Gabi, who was glaring at him. "And underneath - only I knew."

"Brains met brawn." she retorted, with an unladylike snort.

"But - you were flying that plane..." Paul added hastily, "and quite well, may I say."

"Yes - my second career as a bush pilot." she said ironically. "I haven't practiced medicine since I left the military six years ago."

"What I want to know," she pursed her lips in thought. "Is whether it will do it again, or if that was a one-time shot."

"You mean you think we've been infected with some bug that is healing us?" Paul grinned. "Wait 'til I tell the guys I have an alien virus! Cool!"

"No, no, almost certainly not a virus. Virus use our cells to reproduce themselves, not to make more of our cells. Virus are nasty little beggars. Some kinds will transform cells into virus factories, and force them to make more and more viruses until the cell explodes."

"Yuch." Paul made a face.

"No, I am not sure what this is. And I am a bit out of touch," she apologized with a shrug.

"I think you would have heard about something that induces rapid healing." Jed commented drily.

"So is it safe to conclude that the dust did it?" Paul asked.

"Well... I hate to say for sure..."

Jed offered an aside to Paul "Never try to pin her down until she's ready to give an answer"

"It seems like an awfully rapid onset," Gabi ignored him.

"See?"

"And what would actually affect us this way? And not only those of us with an injury, but Jed says he was sick last night, too."

"What did I say?" Jed continued, smirking.

"It's a germ." offered Paul, with an impish smile.

Gabi rolled her eyes and laughed. "You two are impossible."

"So, what are our plans?" Jed asked.

Paul shrugged. "Wait to be rescued?"

"I have a functioning ELT. And the Beaver is pretty noticeable."

"What is an ELT?" Paul asked.

"A Emergency Location Transmitter. Once oh, about twenty-four hours have passed and someone notices that I haven't come back, they'll start looking for me. Not for you guys, because you're supposed to be out here for three more days anyway. Once they start to look for me, they'll fly my filed flight pattern, out to the lake, and then up to Fairbanks, where I was supposed to take you lot. From there, they will start flying parallel to my flight path, expanding outward until they find us."

"Won't that take a while?"

"I hope not. I don't think we are too far off the flight path."

Jed came back from a trip for firewood and added, "I think I saw a logging road or something about the time I took over the controls."

"A kind of wide dirt road?"

"Yes."

"That is the Taylor Highway." She chuckled. "Not that I blame you for thinking that, but it is the main route to Dawson and Eagle. We probably aren't too far from Chicken, as a matter of fact."

"Chicken?"

"They found gold there, and wanted to name it after the most abundant bird... but none of them could spell ptarmigan."

"Gabi, have you given any thought to the consequences of our friendly healing germ?"

"No, what did you have in mind?"

"Quarantine. They're going to lock us up and throw away the key."

Paul put in his two cents worth "They can't keep us forever, and it isn't like we're wildly contagious or something."

"No, I don't think it is contagious, but they will want to figure out how we healed so quickly." She turned to Jed, and he could see the worry in her eyes. "That means the Institute will get involved, and that is a problem for me."

He nodded, grimly. "I thought it would be."

"The Institute? and why is it a problem?"

"The US Army Research Institute of Infectious Diseases. I worked there for a while. My former boss had a... thing about me."

She sat, lost in thought, for a moment. Then she bent her head forward, almost to her knees, running her fingers through her hair. She shuddered. What had she gotten them in for? She had kept track of her former boss, as he had risen in importance, and knew that he was very politically powerful now. Add this to his vendetta against her, and they would all be guinea pigs for the rest of their lives. She, for one, had no intentions of living for any length of time in a military installation again. She did not think Jed would put up with it for long, although he would try, tied to the military as he was, and she had no idea about Paul.

"So, Paul, how do you feel about lab rats?"

Evasions

Jed scanned the former campsite with a practiced eye. It was obvious to him that someone had been there, but not whom, or how many. He had done his best, and now could only hope to fool the rescuers who would come after them. Gabi was swimming back in from the center of the lake. She had used the explosives in his pack to set charges on the airplane, and then towed it out to the center, into deeper water. Now she walked, dripping, out of the water into the marshy edges and gave him a thumbs-up. He nodded, and triggered the blast. It was surprisingly small, as he had made the charges little, just enough to do the job. The plane crumpled sideways and slowly turned turtle, one pontoon still showing. Now the three of them turned their backs on it and walked into the forest.

They had not intended to sink the plane, just to give the impression that the landing had been a lot harder than it really had been. Also, Gabi had wanted to wash out all the gray dust. All of them hoped that their would-be rescuers would give it only a cursory glance before deciding that they had washed out of the plane and were in the lake somewhere. The three of them knew they couldn't run forever, but they wanted to do this on their own terms, and that meant finding out from the aliens what the gray dust had done to them.

But for now they faced a greater difficulty, one that at least Paul had not expected, Jed was sure. Calmly, Jed took point, and pushed his way through the spruce boughs. As the trees grew, and shut off more and more light from one another, the lower branches died. These branches never fell off, but remained perpetually stiff and prickly, making navigation between the crowded trees painful. Gabi, behind Paul, commented "There was a fire through here about twenty-five years ago. That is why all this is so uniform and nasty. Older forest is a lot more clear, and much easier."

"Ouch." Jed nursed a scratch on the back of his hand. "Well, at least we still feel the pain."

"It'll be a lot easier once we find one of the old 'cat' trails." Gabi assured them.

"What?" Paul asked, dodging a branch Jed let go of too soon.

"The trail that were made by miners, a couple of generations ago. They brought in big bulldozers and just cleared a path to where they needed to go. The forest up here grows back slowly, so we will find one easily."

"But that's horrible! How could they cause such damage?"

"What damage?"

"Well, to the trees, and the wildlife..." He fluttered his hands in a gesture no doubt meant to be inclusive of all their surroundings, but hampered by his caution of the spiny branches.

"I don't know about the trees, but the wildlife love it. The moose only eat underbrush, and in heavy forest like this, they go hungry, or move. But they are what has kept those trail open all this time. All that fresh, young growth..." she sidestepped Paul and caught up with Jed. "They eat it every year and the brush never has a chance to move on to the forest stage." To Jed, she remarked, offhandedly. "Rutting season."

"Oh, sh..." he stopped himself. He knew Gabi disliked swearing, but the thought of rambling around in the brush with an angry bull moose was intimidating, even to him.

She shrugged. "I have my forty-four, and I'm sure you have something. I'd rather not use my pistol, as it about takes my wrist apart, but it will stop either a moose or a bear."

He looked dubiously at her, walking beside him now in the open forest. Paul still trailed behind them. "Are you accurate with it?" he asked in curiosity. She nodded. All he could see was the top of her head, her red hair dim in the shadow of the trees.

"Dad makes me take it out every month and use up a box of ammo. He says it'll do me no good at all if I can't hit the broad side of a barn."

"Good. I hope to meet your Dad one of these days. He sounds like my kinda guy." He checked his compass. Down here under the forest canopy it would be all too easy to get lost, with no landmarks, and no way of seeing any. You could not even climb a tree to see where you were going, as the spruce were much too slender at the top to hold a man. The term 'trackless wilderness' applied perfectly to this place, he reflected. Earlier, on his way to the crash site, he had carried an alien beacon that had guided him, and had not paid much attention to direction, just to getting through muskeg and forest intact.

"Fortunately, we've had a frost, so the bugs aren't too bad," Gabi commented, breaking into his reverie.

"Yep," he agreed, increasing his pace. They wanted to make some good time that day, and be far away should their rescuers arrive that day instead of the next.

Tall Tales

They made camp without a fire that night, dining on nuts and berries, as Gabi put it, a trail mix she always kept in the plane for snacking on. Gabi supplemented the meal with handfuls of blueberries that she had picked as they walked along the well-worn moose path. They had kept a sharp eye out for both moose and bear, but had only seen the ubiquitous red squirrels, and twice had heard the crashing of something large moving in the underbrush.

Gabi had kept them all cheerful throughout the day, teaching them to imitate the red squirrels so well that they could irritate the little animals into hanging off branches right over their heads, chittering in indignation and jerking their sparse tails so rapidly that Paul had commented that it was amazing they didn't overbalance themselves. The three of them laughed, joked, and occasionally broke into song as they walked. Gabi knew Jed was keeping a close eye on her, so as they set up camp, she told him quietly, "I haven't felt this good after a hike since I was in highschool. I'm not feeling at all like I was half-dead last night."

He looked at her sharply, evidently not liking her flippant tone, but she pretended to ignore him and unrolled her sleeping bag.

Paul flopped down on his bedroll. "I'm feeling grand. Say, Gabi, do y'think those aliens have something great with this bug, or what? I think everybody in the world is going to want it, once we get back and tell 'em how great it is!"

She shook her head. "I'm not so sure, Paul. I don't know what it is, or how it is affecting our bodies. Also, keep in mind that it made us awfully sick before it made us better. I think the FDA would have something to say about that."

He grinned at her dry tone. "I know people who'd be willing to go through that to become a superman."

Jed broke in. "I think that the problem is two things. One, it is alien technology, and historically, people have been distrustful of change and new technology. Two, the military will want it, and want to keep it under wraps."

"But what if we are contagious or something?"

"Then the military will want to keep us under wraps, too. Why do you think we are running?"

"But I am a civilian, and so is Gabi. Aren't you?" he appealed to her.

Sitting on her sleeping bag , she wrapped her arms around her knees and frowned. "Yes, my stint with the reserves was up two years ago. However, it doesn't matter. We have an 'unknown disease' and they can still quarantine us. However they want to, and it won't matter that we aren't contagious. In this day and age, the thought of an unknown biological running around is going to panic people. I don't know what your alien friends were thinking, Jed, but they might as well have brought a nuke with them to earth. No matter what the benefits might be to us, here, today, who knows what the future will bring."

She stopped and drew a deep breath. The tight feeling in her chest was an old, familiar feeling, but one she had not had in years. She was afraid. The last times she had felt this way were when she had confronted the Hanta virus for the first time, and the last interview with her old boss, Dr. Lewiston.

"So what are we going to do?" Paul asked, now sounding concerned.

"E and E." Jed replied in a joking tone.

"Huh?"

"Escape and evasion." Gabi supplied. "What is the plan, Jed?" She knew he would have a plan. He was trained to think on his feet, to imagine the worst and then plan to survive it and get the mission done.

"I get you guys to town, then get to base and report in. Talk to the alien and figure out what they have done to us, and hopefully, if it is benign, that'll be the end of it. No-one need ever know you and Paul were involved in the incident."

Gabi threw up her hands. "And how are you going to explain the missing Major Guptill, not to mention my plane, and what is supposed to have happened to Paul?"

"There was an accident, we hiked out because I was too impatient to wait for rescue, and then you guys went home. I'm sure the authorities will want to talk to you about the crash. but at least the alien artifact can be suppressed. The military will want it that way anyway."

"That has holes you could drive a truck through." was her dubious reply.

"The colonel will fix it." Jed stated confidently.

"What about the fact that we all have an alien 'germ'?"

"I will talk to the aliens about that." he said grimly. "Paul, I want you and Gabi to stay put once you get to Gabi's home, and wait for me to get back with you."

Gabi nodded. She knew it wasn't perfect, but she also saw what Jed was trying to do. To keep her out of the hands of Dr. Lewiston. She only hoped they succeeded. She didn't think she

could come out of another long session
with Lewiston with her sanity intact.

   She yawned, and said, "How about we
get some sleep? I'm bushed."

   Jed nodded his agreement. She could
barely see his face in the deepening
twilight. He lay down, as did Paul, and
she heard his soft snores a few moments
later. She lay awake watching the
appearing stars, brilliant in the sky
above her, wondering what was out there,
and what harm it could do. All her
professional career she had worried about
things of earth. She had foreseen
resistant strains of diseases appearing
about twenty years before, and the rise
of AIDS had always been with her, as the
first case was found a few years before
her birth. She had seen the discovery of
more hemorrhagic viruses than she cared
to remember, but now the greatest threat
was completely unknown, and it unnerved
her. She closed her eyes and felt sleep
creep over her brain.

   She slept badly, seeing faces in her
dreams that she thought were long
forgotten, faces of her own patients, and
those she had seen only in clinical
photos. She awoke into the frosty night
with a gasp, sitting up and clutching her
throat with one hand. "Gabi." Jed
murmured. She felt more than saw him,
moving toward her. His outline blotted
out the stars overhead as he leaned over

her, them he was holding her, and she clung to his warm frame with a shudder of relief. To her horror, she realized that she was crying.

He didn't say a word, just lifted her into his lap and held her, stroking her hair with his free hand. She didn't dare speak and reveal that she was crying, so she buried her face in the rough fabric of his uniform and let the tears flow silently. After what seemed like a long while, the tears stopped, and she lifted her head. "S-sorry." she managed.

She could feel the chuckle rumble in his chest. "No need to be sorry, bawbee."

She smiled at the scottish term of endearment. "I don't know what's gotten into me."

"I do. I won't let that so and so get his mitts on you again."

"No, no, I'm worried about something else. We already have so many things to worry about here on our own planet, how could they come down and add another set of them? Why are they here? It's not like we were going to notice that they were out there any time soon if we hadn't already. Oh, I could just give them a piece of my mind!"

Jed was overcome with laughter at her indignant speech, and tried in vain to keep his voice down so he would not awaken their sleeping companion. "Oh,

Gabi, I believe you would! I hope to see it someday!"

Paul snorted and rolled over in his sleep, and Jed whispered. "How about we discuss this in the morning? Do you think you can sleep now?"

"Yes, I guess so." her voice was rather stiff after his laughter, but it softened as she added, "thank you."

Escaping

The morning dawned overcast and cool. Gabi cast an approving eye at the lowering cloud cover, and announced cheerfully "This ought to slow them down some. They may not even begin the search yet, thinking maybe I've stopped in somewhere to sit it out."

"Wouldn't they expect you to radio in?"

"No, Paul, there is a lot of country out here where there isn't any way to get out a signal. Too many hills between here and home. I remember Uncle Jim telling me about an accident up on the Taylor Highway, almost to Eagle. It was a bad one - a bus full of senior citizens went off the road and rolled down an embankment. The buss stopped only a few feet short of a seven-hundred foot cliff, held only by a couple of small trees. Once they found it and had to call in the medevac chopper, someone had to drive up to the top of the next hill to get any signal worth using. Uncle Jim drove a hundred and twenty miles responding to that one."

"Wow." Paul responded. " I can't believe it. It makes me think how really wild it is around here."

"Yes, it is, and you can't forget it," she warned, "or this country will swallow you up without a trace."

As they swung along the trail with long strides , Gabi reflected that the second day was faster going, perhaps because of the clearer trail, but Gabi thought it was also because she had said in the morning that they ought to reach the highway by evening, and perhaps even Chicken. Even so, as the day wore on she felt more and more tension. What if the 'germ' as Paul had so handily termed it, really was contagious? Could she countenance exposing anyone, and most especially her friends and family, to it? Wouldn't it be better to just put herself into the hands of the military and trust them to take care of herself and her husband and their new friend?

Finally she voiced her concerns to Jed, who was at point, as usual. He did not turn his head to look back, but she could tell he was thinking about the problem. Finally, he spoke, still without turning his head. "I still think we had better talk to the aliens first. I am dedicated to the Army - you know that, better than anyone - but I don't want this germ to become a weapon, and I don't know what the aliens intended, either."

He stopped for a minute, and Paul asked "Did you get to see them? The aliens, I mean."

"No, nor talk to them, directly. I heard a computer generated voice when speaking with them. I was told that they aren't capable of producing human speech. But I have a hunch that we can trust them..."

"Trust his hunches, " Gabi put in. "His Colonel once told me he'd trust one of Jed's hunches with his life."

"Really?" Jed asked, actually stopping and turning around to see her. "Old Robin actually said that?"

"Yes, he did, dear"

Gabi laughed at his expression of pleasure. After a second, he turned and began to walk again, muttering "Well what do you know..."

In the late afternoon, as the sun sank down behind them, they heard howling in the distance. Paul started nervously, and asked "Are there wolves around?"

"Probably." Gabi answered him without turning her head.

"Aren't you worried about them?"

"No. Wolves, as a rule, don't attack humans. I only know of one documented case in the US where a pack did kill a man, and that was on a remote island in Southeast Alaska."

"Really? Somehow I thought it was more common than that." He was edging closer up behind her, she realized, and she started to talk to calm him down.

"Yeah. When my Uncle Jim was in college, he and his team of surveyors went out onto the island, preparatory to the logging company that owned the lumber on it coming in. There were some rudimentary roads, and they set up camp on one side of these. They were out on the other side, working their way home one afternoon, when they suddenly realized that they were surrounded by a pack. These college boys made a ring and backed slowly away, holding their chainsaws out in front of them, revving them. They edged their way back toward the road, and about the time they got to it, they were pretty worried about the saws running out of gas. But the crew boss had gotten worried, and he and the rest of the crew came up on them at the edge of the road and drove off the wolves."

"Whew. Is that a true story?"

"Yes, and there's more. A couple of nights later they got into camp and it looked like a whirlwind had hit it. Those wolves had come in and investigated pretty much anything in camp - tore it all to pieces. Uncle Jim told me that they even bit canned food, and punctured the cans with their teeth, they were that strong. But the funny thing was, in the center of the camp, they discovered everything decorated liberally with blue and yellow paint. See, they used cans of spray paint in their work, and the wolves had bitten those, too. They never did see the wolves the rest of their time there, but it will still make Uncle Jim chuckle, thinking about those blue and yellow wolves."

Now Jed laughed, and so did Paul. Gabi just smiled. She had heard that story so many times it was an old familiar one to her.

They had been so absorbed in her story that the road came as a surprise to them. They walked out of the narrow green trail they had been following into bright sunlight and dust. Gabi squinted for a moment, looking down at the highway. They stood at the top of a deep cut that had been made for the road, and she could see that getting down onto the road would be annoying. They had a choice of traveling down the hill parallel to the road, fighting through the thick brush that grew there - which included, she thought, some Devil's club - or of sliding down the steep embankment on their derrieres. With a sigh, she resigned herself to the latter, undignified method. It might hurt her pride, but it was better than tangling with a brushy patch of a plant that was covered in inch long spines.

She lowered herself into a sitting position, hearing Paul mutter in disbelief behind her.

"Here goes!" and she was off, sliding down the dusty, rocky slope until it leveled off a few feet from the road. She stood up and watched Jed and Paul sliding awkwardly after her. She greeted them with a laugh and a hand up.

"So, Gabi, which way to Chicken?" Paul asked as he attempted to get most of the dust off. He looked up and down the narrow dirt road as he asked, obviously trying to figure out where they were.

"This is a highway?" Jed grinned as he scuffed his toe in the well-packed road surface. "Not bad, for a dirt road."

"Hey! my Dad helped build part of this!" she protested, but added, smiling, "Well, it is closed every year from October to April."

"As for your question, Paul, Chicken is to the south of us now, so let's get going. I should be able to call for a ride from there. Stay to the side of the road." she warned.

"Why?"

"Because the damtourists pay no attention to the fact that there are a lot of animals wandering around these parts, and they go whipping through here, looking to be killed."

"Oh. Okay"

They fell quickly into the pattern of walking they had developed over the past few days. Jed took point, his eyes never down, obviously aware of everything

around them. Gabi followed, and Paul
brought up the rear. He was distracted
several times by the layers of rock
exposed in the cut they were walking
through, and periodically Gabi would have
to call to him to remind him to catch up.
Finally, she told him in exasperation
that he was worse than a child to keep
track of.

"Do you have any kids, Gabi?" he
asked, walking beside her now. She looked
away from him, feeling the old, familiar
pain at the thought of children. "Sorry,
I can see it's something you don't want
to talk about."

"No, it's ok. Kids just never...
happened. Now," she shrugged. "It might
not be too late, I guess."

Jed turned around at this and fixed
her with a piercing gaze. "Paul, why
don't you keep going, and Gabi and I will
catch up."

He looked startled, from one to the
other, but then shrugged and obediently
kept walking.

"Gabi," Jed came so close to her that
she could see the lines at the corners of
his eyes. "Gabi, I can't not tell you
this, but I can't have kids."

"Why?" she felt tears welling up in
her eyes, and blinked them back, not
wanting to show her emotions."

He shrugged, looking very unhappy.
"After we split up, I had a vasectomy. I

was afraid I'd get you pregnant, and you would be stuck raising a child on your own. Oh, I knew I'd give you as much support as I could, but I also knew that I'd be gone a lot, and..." his voice trailed off, and he just stood there, looking miserable, for a long moment. Then, softly, "Can you forgive me?"

"Yes." Gabi reached up and touched his cheek, bristly now even though he had shaved before they left camp that morning. "I understand. But maybe we could adopt after this all gets straightened out?"

He beamed. "Yes, that is a wonderful idea. And, Gabi, I want you to know that my time is up in about a month, and I will not re-enlist."

She gasped. "But Jed, it isn't..."

He put a hand over her mouth. "It isn't my life anymore." He said simply.

Then he turned around and marched off with his long strides, leaving her standing breathless on the side of the road.

She walked slowly toward the men, who were disappearing round the corner, her mind in a turmoil.

As she rounded the corner, though, everything was swept from her mind. There was a Suburban pulling over by the guys, who had obviously flagged it down. She walked up next to Jed and smiled at the driver. Then she realized that she knew him, and her smile brightened. "Why, Mr. Peabody, what are you doing up this way?"

"Came up looking for a good spot to camp when caribou season kicks off. Also, I wanted to go fishing. The missus went to Fairbanks, so I was sorta lonely." His eyes twinkled, and his teeth flashed behind the short beard he wore. Gabi recognized it as the beginnings of his winter growth.

"What about the Trading Post?" she inquired after his store, located just twenty miles from the Canadian border, the first stop for anyone crossing over into Alaska. He shrugged

"Put up a 'gone fishin' sign. Planned on going home tomorrow, anyways. Say, what are you doing up here? And where's your truck?"

"Well, actually, it was my plane, and it's at the bottom of a lake thataway." she gestured in the direction they had come from.

"Holy sh... Sorry, Gabi." he too had been on the receiving end of her sharp comments about cursing, a view shared by his wife.

"Wasn't my best day, no. Could you give us a lift to Chicken? Then I'll call my Dad for a ride."

"Well, sure, but you can just ride home with me. No sense in him coming up here if I'm already here."

"All right." Gabi didn't mind sparing her father the hundred and fifty mile round trip.

"Well, climb on in!"

With that all three of them piled in, Jed and Paul in the back, Gabi into the front. Gabi introduced them two men with her to Mr. Peabody, who twisted around and shook hands jovially with each of them.

"You don't have to call me Mr. Gabi's known me since she was a mite of a thing, and can't get used to anything else, I guess. Call me Gary."

"Good to meet you, then. Gabi didn't mention it, but I am also her husband." Jed added, as he shook the proffered hand. Then he regretted it, as the twinkle in Gary's eyes disappeared and he gripped Jed's hand hard enough to make even the special forces soldier wince.

"Really."

"Yes. We're getting back together." Gabi supplied, turning around to see Jed rubbing his hand once he'd gotten it back. She chuckled at his chagrined look.

He muttered "Guess I deserved that."

"Yes, you did, young man. But now that you mention it, Gabi does look happier then I've seen her in a while."

He started the engine, introductions over, and expertly maneuvered the big truck around and set off to the south again. Gabi chatted with their host for a few moments about his family, as she hadn't seen them in a couple of months, but she was lulled by the motion of the vehicle and soon was struggling to stay awake. Gary saw her fighting the sleep off and said "Get some rest. Appears all of you are tuckered out."

Gabi looked back and realized that both Jed and Paul were soundly asleep, Paul curled up in his seat like a child, and Jed leaned back against the seat, with his mouth agape. Smiling, she settled herself comfortably and closed her eyes.

Old Soldiers

When Jed awakened he was stiff, but not as sore as he would have expected. He leaned forward to see Gabi, asleep against the door. Gary turned his head for a brief smile, then returned to concentrating on the road. They were turning off, Jed realized. The change in speed must have been what had awakened him. The cloud of dust caught up with them, briefly, and when it had settled Jed could see a sprawling log building, with a sign proclaiming it to be the Forty-Mile Road house. Gabi stirred, but did not awaken, and Paul simply snorted.

Gary looked at Jed, "Need a pit stop ?"

"Um, sure." he was surprised at the rasp in his voice. "And some water, I think."

As they walked into the roadhouse, Gary kept looking at Jed, but he did not speak. Jed also looked at this friend of his wife's. A big man, easy in this rough environment, and with a somewhat intimidating manner to most, Jed guessed. Jed thought he saw a hint of former soldier in the way the man moved.

As they stood at the counter, Jed asked quietly, "Where did you serve?"

Gary shot him a sharp look, and waited until they were back outside in the crisp fall air to answer. "Well, I ought to have guessed you'd pick up on that. I was with her Dad in Nam. I'm not gonna talk about it, not even to you."

Jed nodded. "No, I wouldn't ask. Just... curious."

"So, what are you? Gabi only ever said you were in the Army. I thought she'd married someone she worked with, but..." Gary looked him up and down, assessing Jed shrewdly.

"Airborne Ranger."

Gary stopped, stared a second, then let out a whistle. He shoved out his hand and Jed took it wordlessly. Then he looked down at the well-worn coin in the palm of his hand with a chuckle. "I might have guessed!" He laughed out loud as he passed the coin back. "Gabi's Dad, too?"

"Nope. He drove us around, you might say."

The twinkle was back in the big man's eyes. "Well, now, why did you let Gabi get away from you?"

Jed spread his hands in a gesture of helplessness. "I only know one way of fighting a battle , and to keep on as we were would have been really bad for her. She needed to get away from the Army, and I... I guess I was young and dumb, sir."

"Did you ever hurt her."

He asked calmly, not looking at Jed, but Jed knew he had to answer the right way, or his life would be a shorter one. They were standing still in the middle of the parking lot, Gary gazing down at the Alaska Highway, and Jed looking at him, hands folded behind his back. "No, never. Not physically. I was afraid I would, though." he admitted.

"You did better than I, boy."

Gary looked at Jed, his brown eyes bleak. "I hit my lovely bride just once, and she..." He raised his arm and showed Jed the long scar that ran from wrist to elbow. "She'd have killed me if she could have gotten past my guard. But I never raised a hand to her again, and I retired the week after, and we came up here to be close to Lew. That's why I ask. I know how it can be, to go from fighting a war to fighting your wife, and to cross that line."

"Yes. That is why I let her go. I was afraid of myself."

The two men smiled at one another. Then Gary slapped Jed on the back, eliciting a grunt from the younger man. "'Nough male bonding. Let's get you home!"

Gabi yawned and sat up when they opened the doors. "Hey." she greeted them blearily.

"Need a bathroom? At least stretch your legs."

"Yeah." she yawned again.

"Paul?"

"All right, I'm coming too."

His sandy brown hair was sticking all up one one side, but he rubbed his face with both hands and climbed out of the vehicle. He caught up with Gabi, and she spoke to him as they went into the store, but Jed was too far away to hear what she said.

"So do you have any children, Gary?"

"Yep. Five of them. Four boys and a girl. The eldest is about Gabi's age. None of them are married, though." he sighed. "I wonder if we'll ever have grand babies."

"What do they do? I gathered you have a store."

"Well, Tab helps out with the store, and her brothers run a guide camp out toward Denali a ways. They come in for the winter, and we keep a bunkhouse for them. It gets rowdy, sometimes." he snorted. "How about you? Any family?"

"No, I was an only child and I lost my parents in a car accident the year before I married Gabi. I have some cousins in Scotland, but I haven't seen them since I was a lad."

Gabi and Paul got back to them then, and climbed in, both looking brighter." Ready to go? All right then."

As they drew closer to Tok, Gabi would periodically point out landmarks,

but Jed watched her closely. Her position
in front of him enabled him to watch her
without her knowledge. He was wondering
whether she would regret what she had
said about rebuilding their marriage. She
had a good life up here, secure with her
family and friends around her. He thought
that adding an old soldier to her life
might not be a good thing. Hell, he
didn't know anything else but the Army,
and a part of the Army that didn't
translate to civilian life well, at that.
So what was he going to do with himself
when he got out? There was that guide
camp Gary's boys owned... Jed figured he
could shoot, all right, and he could find
his way around, too. But it sounded like
it was a ways away... he would like not
to uproot Gabi. Maybe she would rather he
wasn't around all that often, anyway.

As he pursued this line of thought,
growing ever more unsure of himself, he
fell asleep again.

Gabi grew silent after they passed
through the town. Jed was watching her
again, and he could see that she was
thinking. Finally she asked "Gary, could
you please take me to my house first? I
want to get a shower and I'll call Carl
about the plane from there before I go to
Dad's"

"All right. I don't think anyone
knows you went down yet, or Lewis would
have called us. Otherwise I'd take you

right home, young lady." He gave her a glare, which she returned with a smile.

"Yes, Uncle Gary."

Shortly, they turned off the Alaska Highway onto a well maintained gravel road. They bounced along that for a mile or so, until finally turing into the driveway of a tiny log house with a sod roof.

Gabi tumbled out of the truck and waved her arm at it. "Home, Sweet Hut! Come in and I'll put the coffee on."

Jed looked around the open interior with a fascinated gaze. He estimated the house dimensions to be perhaps twenty feet by sixteen, and there were no interior walls. Her bed was sequestered by a canopy, but the rest of the house centered around the woodstove that stood in the middle on a raised hearth. He was just beginning to wonder if there was an indoor bathroom when Gabi opened a door he had noticed in the rear of the house and indicated it.

"I finally got electricity out here last year and Dad helped me build this. It gets chilly in the winter because the only heat is from the stove, but it is nice to not have to heat and carry water for a shower. Paul, you want first dibs?"

"Sure thing!"

"Towels are on the shelf. Help yourself. Hmmm..." she looked him up and down for a minute. "I think I can find something for you to wear."

"Okay. I'm really looking forward to being clean!"

As he closed the door, Gabi opened the bottom drawer under her raised bed. Jed came and leaned on the corner post, looking at it, and her.

"Bed fit for a princess. High enough to need a little stool to get into, canopied... Seems a lot like the one you always wanted."

"Yes. I built it for myself when I finished up the cabin."

"I'm sorry. I wanted to build one like this for you."

She sat back on her heels and looked up at him. Her hair was falling out of the ponytail she had hastily put it into that morning, and he reached down to brush it out of her eyes. Her hands were full of clothes, so she smiled at him, and said only "Maybe someday you will have a chance."

Gary, standing by the sink and opening cupboards, interrupted them, asking "Gabi, where do you keep your coffee?"

Standing, she tucked the bundle of clothes under one arm. Then she went to his side and pulled the coffee out from behind something in the cabinet he was looking in.

"Oh, yeah." He looked sheepish.

She laughed, "I don't care, as long as you're makin' the coffee."

Jed chuckled and looked around the tiny kitchen. The sink was in front of a window that looked out at the woods beside the house. Above the sink, her plates and bowls rested in a rack. He recognized the deep blue glazed stoneware. To each side hung a single cabinet over a short counter. In the corner was an insulated box that he guessed had been her refrigerator until she got electricity, as there was now a short frig on a stand next to it. After the refrigerator, the wall was lined with bookshelves crammed full of books, until they reached the bed in the far corner. Next to the bed was a handbuilt armoire to hang clothes in, he guessed again, and then her tiny sitting area, a loveseat and a chair, facing the wood stove. In the corner by the door were pegs for coats and hats, and a special low shelf for boots and shoes. As Jed slowly surveyed all this, he was leaning against the little table that served as her desk, dining table, and kitchen workspace. Three chairs around it led him to speculate that her only frequent visitors were her uncle and father. Finally he looked at Gabi, who was smiling at him. He recognized her expression as insecurity.

"I really like it. It is cozy, but efficient-looking. You have made it very homey."

"Thank you. Here," and she thrust a stack of clothes into his hands. He looked at them, as she took another stack to the bathroom for Paul. A battered pair of BDU trousers, his own, he realized, a garish T-shirt, and even a pair of underwear, although he had no idea how she had ended up with a pair of his underwear - and they were surely his, for they had 'McGregor' on the waistband, as he had been marking them for years, so his laundry service couldn't lose them. Shrugging, he looked up to see Gary watching him.

"A little primitive, even for you?"

"No," Jed said with a shake of his head. "I like it very much. I've stayed in worse places, and this could be a lovely home."

Gary snorted "Two people certainly have to be in tune with one another to live in one room together."

"True."

Gabi tapped Jed on the shoulder, and he looked around in surprise. Her cheeks were rosy, and her hair wet. "your turn," she announced.

"Is there any hot water?"

"Yes, I have an on-demand heater. Great for those long showers I love."

He laughed and made his way into the little room. She had put it into a shed off the back of the house, and he had to duck a little to get his head under the showerhead, but it felt awfully good to get clean again. He found a razor laid out next to the sink, and realized a moment later that he was whistling cheerfully as he scraped his face smooth. He stopped a minute and grinned at his reflection. "I could get used to this, although I'll have to buy a flexible head for the shower. As soon as I go back and deal with the aliens, I get to come home to... her."

Finished a few minutes later, he entered the other room to find it crowded with two more people.

"Jed, I'd like you to meet my Dad, and Uncle Jim."

Jed stepped forward, hand extended, and met her father. Lewis Charranau was a short man, but wiry and obviously tough. His thinning black hair was kept cut very short in a style Jed recognized as Marine. "Hello, I'm Lewis." he greeted Jed shortly, and Jed knew he had some convincing to do here. He did not resent it, though. He knew he had earned the suspicion of her father. Then he turned to the other man, who looked much like his brother, only shaggier. Uncle Jim sported a full, bushy beard, and a shiny pate. He grinned and shook without speaking.

Gabi heaved a sigh. "Well, now that you are here... You might as well hear the whole story. Uncle Gary, should you call Aunt Nia?"

He waved this off. "She won't be home until tomorrow, and I wouldn't miss this."

"You guessed there was more to the story?"

He chuckled at her sheepish expression. "Yeah, I figured there had to be a reason for you all to leave that plane and then not to notify Carl right away."

She grimaced at mention of her boss, and then invited them all to sit. Her father rather pointedly maneuvered himself next to her on the couch, and Jed found himself on one of the kitche chairs across from them. He watched as Gabi snuggled her father, and wished momentarily that they had had children. Wouldn't it have been lovely to have a child who would love _him_ like that?

Gabi cleared her throat and prompted, "Jed, I believe the story starts with you?

Later, as Gabi wrapped the story up with their meeting with Gary Peabody, Jim chuckled. "Darn if that doesn't rival any of mine. I take my hat off to you, girl.

Now, how are we going to explain all of this to Carl?"

She smiled at him, and Jed felt a rush of relief as he realized that not only had they been believed, but the three men were going to help them untangle this mess. Then the phone rang,and all of them looked around quickly.

Gabi answered it. "Yes? yes, I did have a crash, Carl. I'm just at home getting ready to come tell you all about it... There are four men there asking about me?"

Jed stood up and took two steps toward her, all his instincts blazing danger at him. Then Gabi stiffened, and she said only "Understood. I will be gone in less than five minutes, can you keep them that long?" After an instant, she finished with "I owe you one," and hung up.

Jed was already collecting his dirty clothes and telling Paul in a low voice to do them same when she turned to face them. "Carl told me he wants me to get out of town. He thinks something is wrong about these guys, and he says they aren't military."

Her father stood. "What do you want me to do?"

"Just go home, and stay there until I let you know. These people have no Idea any of you are here, and while I don't know for sure anything is wrong, I would just as soon you were all safe at home. Go, Dad."

He looked at her for a minute longer, his brow furrowed, obviously weighing his options, before hugging her and saying, "Call as soon as you can. You know I worry."

Gabi stopped Gary at the door and handed him a flash drive. He looked at it briefly, understanding dawning on his face, and then shoved it in his pocket. He grabbed her shoulders and growled "You take care of yourself, mind?"

She nodded. Every muscle in her body felt tight, coiled like a spring. She submitted to his hug, then shoved him away. "Go home, straight home and don't talk to anyone about this. Keep the tape, but don't use it, for Heaven's sake. No-one will believe you yet. I- I think you'll know when it is time. Jed and Paul and I are the ones they are after right now. Let's keep it that way, all right?"

"All right."

Gabi ran the rest of the way to her own vehicle. Jed and Paul had already climbed in, and she saw that Jed had grabbed some food and drinks out of the house. Gabi threw the three-day pack into the back of the pickup and climbed in the driver's side. "Ready?" she asked, looking at Jed, then in the rearview mirror at Paul in the backseat. Paul looked a little pale, but otherwise calm.

"Let's go." Jed said. "Is there a back way out of here?"

"Well, there is the Tetlin trail, but it's pretty rough."

"Can your truck handle it?"

"I think so!" she laughed. Her adrenaline was running so high that she was ready to try anything.

A few minutes later Jed was clutching the handle above the passenger window and looking rather surprised. "Jesu... Gabi, this is more than just rough!"

"Nah... just a touch bumpy." She teased as she swerved hard to avoid a particularly bad set of ruts. They were driving down a narrow path, flanked by think spruce forest, and delineated by deep ruts, obviously created by ATV's, as they were too narrow for the truck. Branches occasionally scraped the sides of the truck as the trees closed in, but Gabi knew this section of the trail quite well, and she knew that it was passable all the way to the highway. As she drove, she thought through their next moves. After they got back on the highway, there was nowhere to turn off for a hundred miles. She would have perhaps ten minutes lead on her pursuers. It wasn't enough.

Jed leaned over, still holding onto the strap, and caressed her cheek. "It will be all right."

Gabi smiled grimly in reply as she swung the truck up onto the Alaska Highway. Once onto the pavement, she accelerated smoothly until the truck was traveling at top speed.

"What are you doing?" Paul cried, clutching for a handhold.

"Buying us some time."

"Won't you get pulled over?"

"I hope not. But there are only two troopers in Tok, and odds are they are looking in the wrong direction."

"Wow, there must be a lot of speeding on these roads then."

She chuckled, a grim sound in the cab of the pickup. "You'd think so, but every year some drunk idiot has a close encounter with a buffalo. Keeps most of us honest, most of the time."

"What about now?"

"Well, hopefully, if a buffalo steps put in the road, we can avoid it."

"Wait," Paul sounded confused. "There are buffalo in Alaska?"

"Yes, a whole herd of the big woolies. They opened up hunting on them a couple years back, they have done so well. Breeding like bunnies."

Her cheerful tone made Jed smile – she could see him out of the corner of her eye. He hadn't said a word, and she was grateful for that. This was his area of expertise, and she knew if she asked he'd advise her, but for now she needed to stay focused.

It wasn't until they were ten miles out of Delta Junction and she started to slow down that she saw the big pick-up truck in her rearview mirror. She looked at it for a moment, then pulled her eyes back to the road and tried to ignore it. Jed and Paul both turned and looked back at it, then looked at her.

"Any ideas?" she asked lightly.

"Could it have come from that little Indian village back there?"

"Tanacross? Yes, but I don't think so. I think it is our friends from town."

She looked again and the truck was still accelerating, gaining on them rapidly. She turned off the highway onto a little dirt road, startling the men by her sudden decision and by the velocity of the turn.

"Where are we headed?" Jed asked once he'd gotten his breath back.

"To Oscar's place. He has a little plane I'm sure he'll let me use. Are they following us?"

"Um..." Paul was kneeling on the back seat now, peering out the rear window, trying to see through the dust.

"No, I don't think so."

"Good, maybe it wasn't them."After another ten minutes Gabi swung the truck into a long, winding drive that ended in front of a ramshackle cabin. She stopped and rested her forehead on the steering wheel for a moment, her shoulders sagging. Jed reached over and rubbed her neck for a moment, looking absently around. She felt his hand stop moving, and sensed his increased alertness by the sudden tension in his body. She lifted her head and saw Oscar standing in his door.

He was, as usual with visitors, holding a shotgun on them, scowling grimly. His long white hair bristled wildly atop his head and he looked like he hadn't shaved in a week. Jed and Paul, were eyeing him with some alarm. Gabi grinned as she opened the door and slid out.

"Put it up, you old coot. I'm too tired to deal wi' your nonsense."

"Gabrielle!" he shouldered the weapon and came down off the porch, his tall, thin body stiffening into the erect, military posture she had come to expect from him. "My dear," taking her hand and kissing it lingeringly, "How delightful of you to drop in. And who are your companions?"

"Oscar, this is Paul Miller, a geologist... at least, I think he is." she eyed Paul, a sudden suspicion popping into her head. She looked at him for an instant, thinking 'I'll ask you about this later,' then moved on. "And this is my husband, Captain Jed McGregor."

"Ah. I am interested to meet you, sir."

Jed looked a little wary, but he shook the proffered hand and smiled politely.

"Now, won't you all come in for a cup of tea?"

They filed after him into the cabin, which was as spartan inside as it appeared outside. Jed let his eyes roam around the single room, but the only thing that caught his interest at all was the rolled up rug in the corner. It had obviously been thrown back from the trapdoor in the floor. He wondered where the door went, but his host was offering them steaming cups of something, so he tore his thoughts away and smiled politely as he took it. With the first sip he almost gagged. "what _is_ this?" he asked, holding the cup further away from him in an instinctive gesture.

"Earl Grey tea. Made my way." Oscar explained simply. "I boil the tea until it is strong enough for my taste. Is it too strong?"

"Errr..." Jed wasn't quite sure what to say.

Gabi interrupted "I need your plane, Oscar."

He raised a bushy eyebrow. "Well, you may not have it."

She drew in a deep breath, but he raised a hand to forestall her. "I have already arranged alternate transport. Why on earth didn't you all stay with the plane when you crashed it?"

Gabi was left staring at him, her mouth hanging open slightly. Jed, too, looked dumbfounded. Only Paul looked slightly uncomfortable. then he cleared his throat.

"Ah... who is coming to get us, exactly?"

"The military, of course. You don't think I would invite the aliens, did you?"

"Weel, it depends on who you are, sir."

"I am..." Oscar drew himself up, back into a military stance. "Captain Damstrake, former RAF. Also, one of the very few humans to be returned intact to Earth after an interrogation by the aliens."

"You were..." Jed choked, then got out "Kidnapped by aliens?"

"Oscar," Gabi interrupted what could be a lengthy conversation. "We were followed from Tok. Four guys in a pick-up. I don't know if they saw us turn onto your driveway, but they'll figure it out before too long."

"Hmmm..." He ran his fingers through his hair, succeeding in making it even wilder than it had been before. "I'd like to meet them, I didn't think our enemies had a presence on Earth right now. Then again, by now everyone involved knows what you three are up to, if not why." He gave Gabi a piercing look. She tried her best to look clueless back at him. "Actually, I think it is probably best you left the plane. If they are this close behind you, they might well have gotten there first, too. Come with me."

He walked over to the trapdoor, and gave it a good, hearty pull. It rose slowly, with the faint hiss of hydraulics. A dim blue-white light spilled into the dim cabin. He started down the stairs, gesturing for them to follow. Paul came last, and yelped and ducked when the door closed almost on his head.

Oscar's safe room was just that, a room about the size of the cabin above, full of odd equipment and other, more familiar things, such as the bed in one corner, and the tiny kitchenette in the other. Oscar made his way to what looked like a flat-topped desk and spread his hands over it, speaking clearly into midair, "Eilson Air Force Base, G'his liaison."

A hologram popped into being under his hands, and he moved them away, revealing an image of a man in military uniform. "Oscar, are they there with you?" The image tried to peer around the room, it seemed.

"Yes, and ready to come into to safety. It seems they were chased out of Tok by four pursuers."

"Oh." The man's expression changed to alarm. "Oscar, I think you had better come in with them, and blow your hidey-hole."

Oscar blinked, then said warily. "I hear you, and I'll do as I see fit."

He waved his hands over the desktop and the hologram disappeared. He looked up at his guests and grinned, suddenly. "You all look like you have exceeded your surprise limit for the day. I can't think when I last saw so many befuddled faces."

Gabi shook herself. "Explain later, I think." she said faintly. "How soon until our ride gets here?"

"Oh, 'bout ten minutes, I think. I'm about sixty air-miles from the base."

Jed nodded. "And we're going to have company before then, or can we stay down here?"

Oscar shook his head. "No, afraid not. They will know your vehicle, and if they are who I think they are, they won't be satisfied until they find you."

He turned his attention to another monitor, and Gabi, looking over his shoulder, could see that it monitored his long drive.

"Ah. There they are, about half-way her, but moving slow."

"So that's the reason for all those potholes." she murmured in his ear. Despite his disheveled appearance, he smelled like lavendar. She sighed. "In all the years I've known you, you never leave anything to chance. So what is the plan now?"

He snorted. "I still want to get a good look at them. It's possible we've gotten our tits in a tizzy for no good reason."

"But you don't think so." This was Jed, from his other side. "Your cabin would be the best place for Gabi and Paul to set up an ambush from."

"And where will you be?"

He came around and gave her a gentle kiss. "No need to get so indignant about it. I'll be in the bushes, where else?"

He hefted what looked like a bundle of rags. "May I?" he asked Oscar.

"Of course. I made it myself, you understand, to better blend in with the local vegetation. Let's get moving now."

Again, he led them up the stairs. They all scrambled after him as quickly as they could, back into the tiny, primitive cabin. Jed donned the ghillie suit and was gone without another word, his face set into harsh, unfamiliar lines. Paul and Oscar went out to the truck to retrieve her rifle, and Gabi checked the rifle Oscar had handed to her.

When he came back in he showed them the shooting holes near the floor, where they could lie on their bellies and look out unseen. Paul whistled in admiration as Oscar pinned back the flap of wood and insulation blocking his off.

"You had planned for a siege, hadn't you?"

"Well, I had the advantage. I knew they were coming."

"What happened to you?"

"A scout ship of the G'his picked me up, and took me out into space. They interrogated me, and had just gotten around to torturing me for the last bits of information I wouldn't give up when another ship showed up and... well, captured them. I still don't know all the details of how they did it. The second set of aliens - the Cats, I called them - brought me back to Earth and set up the Roswell doctrine."

"That long ago?" Paul said in an awed voice.

At the door now, Oscar grinned down at him. "Yep. Only it wasn't a crash in the desert. It was the ship that took me. We brought it back to study, and the Cats took off again."

He slung his shotgun over his shoulder and stepped out onto the porch. Any time now, that truck would come around the bend... There it was.

From her vantage point inside the cabin, Gabi could only see the scuffed heels of Oscar's boots. The rest of him was silent, and she found herself holding her breath as the truck rolled to a stop. The doors opened, and she could see them step out, and then, as they walked closer, she could see their faces better through the dust cloud that was settling around them. They were oddly round-faced. She thought they were almost a caricature of mongloid features, with a pronounced epicanthic fold at the corner of their eyes. Each of them was as like the others, enough so to make her wonder if they were brothers.

"Where are the people who were in this truck?" One of them opened the door of her truck and looked in. His voice was guttural, with a heavy accent Gabi did not recognize.

"That is none of your business, and you can get off my land now." Oscar was gruff enough to frighten away the average intruder, and cocking the shotgun to punctuate his words would have made anyone nervous. These men just focused their combined gaze intently on him and started to walk toward the porch, and Oscar. Oscar himself stepped down off the porch, and met them half-way.

Gabi couldn't hear what Oscar said to them, but for the first time she saw an expression on their faces. A faint gleam of surprise. Then one of them fluidly turned toward the house and drew a weapon, all in one motion. He fired and Oscar fired together. The house seemed to collapse, the central beam falling toward her as she rolled toward the door too late, much too late.

Discoveries

When Gabi woke up she was in a white, sterile looking room. At first she stared at the ceiling for a moment, trying to remember what had happened, then she turned her head. Paul Monroe was sitting in the bed across the room from her, tapping away on a laptop. He noticed she was awake, and smiled cheerfully.

"Hey, welcome back! You gave everyone a bit of a fright, you know."

"Where's," she stopped and cleared her raspy throat. "Where's Jed? and Oscar?"

"I'm not sure where Oscar went, after the dust settled. But he and Jed took out all four bad guys, and then Jed pulled most of the wreckage off us before the helicopter got there. Jed's being debriefed. He ought to be back any minute now." Paul reassured her. "They had to pry him away from you," he added.

Gabi gave him a weak smile. Then she asked politely, "How is your chest?"

"Almost healed!" he exclaimed, gesturing down at the bandage wrapped around the upper half of him. "I can't believe how much better it feels already! How is your head?"

"Well, I have a wicked headache, but..." she gingerly felt the back of her head, and found a small shaved area and a smaller scab. "covered over!"

"How long was I out?" she demanded.

"Just a day! Scout's honor!" he protested at her look of disbelief.

"What is going on?" she asked, wary of their surroundings.

"I'm wondering that too. They quarantined us just like you said they would, then they transported us out of Eilson Air Force Base for points unknown."

They looked at one another for a moment, then Paul asked, tentatively,

"What will they do to us?"

Gabi started to answer, but was interrupted by Jed's appearance in the doorway. He was pale, and held onto the doorframe for support, but at least he was on his feet.

"Jed, what is going on?"

"I think I'll let Doctor Drentz answer that question," he replied, sitting in the chair next to her bed.

A white-coated man with a dark complexion and bright smile strode into the room, holding three charts. "Ah, all here!"

"Now," he said briskly, "There is nothing wrong with any of you. As a matter of fact, there seems to a good deal right. The problem is, we are not entirely sure why. You, young lady" he nodded at Gabi, "and you, sir," directed to Paul, "are healing much more quickly than you ought to be. Mrs. McGregor, you had a hairline fracture of the skull and a nasty laceration when you first arrived, but your most recent x-rays show no sign of it. You were in a coma, but came out of it on your own and seem to be recovering beautifully. I think the only side affect you may notice will be the ragged hair from your previous injury and this one. "

Gabi, putting a hand to the back of her head, grimaced at what she felt.

The doctor continued, with a sympathetic glance. "Your cells seem to be regenerating at an incredible speed. I have never seen anything like it. Also, there is something... odd about your blood. All three of you, you have an unidentified prokaryote swimming your blood stream."

His dry comment made Gabi's skin crawl. This she had not expected. She had fervently hoped that the gray dust had been an external agent, but now, with all of them recovering from the pursuit, she had known that it was not, and having her suspicion confirmed was unpleasant.

Jed lifted his brows "Worms, doctor?"

Doctor Drentz shook his head, "No, tiny little organisms. Approximately the size of your red blood cells. It is possible," he hesitated momentarily, then continued slowly. "It is possible they are responsible for your rapid healing."

Whatever they are," he continued more briskly, "I must ask you to stay for a few more days for observation, even though I think you will both be quite well by tonight. Captain McGregor, you as well." he nodded courteously at Jed, who nodded back.

"Doctor, where are we?" asked Gabi.

The dark little man chuckled, looking positively jolly. "Why, Area 51, my dear!"

"Is there anything I can get for you?" he continued, cocking his head to one side.

Paul and Gabi asked together "Can I get something to eat?"

Paul added, "I'm starved!"

"Yes, yes, certainly, and I will see you in the morning." and the doctor nodded at them all before leaving.

Jed chuckled. "Odd bird, but he does seem to know his stuff."

"Parasites," murmured Gabi to herself, looking thoughtful.

"I'm not sure I like the idea of my blood full of bugs." Paul commented. "But if they help me heal like this, they can't be all bad I guess."

Gabi continued to look concerned. "I was really hoping there would be no internal agent, although I suppose I should be grateful for anything that keeps us alive, especially after that..." she shuddered.

Jed made his way to a chair and lowered himself into it gingerly, obviously still tender from his healing wounds. "I hope they don't keep us long. I want to go home. I am not fond of hospitals."

Paul asked "Was he serious about Area 51?"

"I don't know, I only know it was dark, and a desert. The air smelled dry. We all slept most of the flight." he added thoughtfully. "I' think part of that was our healing - remember before, you two were hungry and sleepy? but I think some of it was... ah - induced."

"You think we were drugged?"

"No, I think it was the parasite." said Gabi, joining the conversation. "I am thinking this through. If the parasite is helping us repair our bodies, it must be drawing on our resources to do so. Hence, sleepiness and hunger. I wonder if it is a parasite, or a simpler organism."

Paul then demanded an explanation of the difference, and she lapsed into lecture mode.

Their conversation was interrupted by the arrival of an orderly with their food. He was accompanied by a second one, who bore clothes for Paul and Gabi. Both orderlies wore surgical masks, and gloves.

Paul and Gabi fell on their food, ravenous, while Jed ate his more slowly.

"Gabi," he said after a few minutes "Did you see...?"

"Yes," she replied, hastily swallowing. "They think it may be contagious."

"What?" asked Paul around a mouthful of food.

Jed answered, as Gabi was eating again. "The parasite we are carrying. I don't think our esteemed medical personnel know what to do about us, and they aren't going to take chances that we will give it to someone else."

"But why didn't Dr. Drentz take those precautions?"

"He may have been exposed to us before they knew what was going on, he may have chosen not to so that he could gain our trust... I have no idea." she sighed in frustration. "Only guesses about... everything."

After they were finished eating, Gabi fell asleep almost immediately. Jed leaned over her, tucking her in and kissing her forehead gently. He turned away to see Paul looking at the other wall self-consciously. Jed walked over and tapped him on the shoulder. Paul looked up, smiling sheepishly.

"Didn't want to intrude." he explained.

"It's all right. I am glad you are the other person involved in this. I think the three of us get along very well." Jed put out his hand, and Paul shook it with a rueful smile.

"You and Mrs. McGregor are good people."

"Please, Jed and Gabi. She always says Mrs. McGregor makes her feel like she's just baked Peter Rabbit into a pie."

Paul laughed, then yawned.

"Good night," chuckled Jed, returning to the armchair beside Gabi's bed and settling in.

The next morning they were escorted to a room full of machines and apparatus. Paul looked around and groaned.

"Why do I get the feeling that today we are supposed to be guinea pigs?"

"Hopefully we will find out what is going on," muttered Gabi.

It was a long day. Individually, and together, they were poked, prodded, and exercised to exhaustion. At noon they all ate a huge meal, discovering that their appetites had doubled. Then they were back on treadmills, where all three of them discovered their stamina had drastically increased. Paul was astonished, for he had never been much of an athlete. That evening, they were taken back to a different place, a suite of rooms that Jed eyed warily, sure they were being watched and listened to. They explored for a moment, finding a hotel-like suite - two bedrooms, a bath, and sitting area. Paul flopped in a chair and asked Gabi,

"Think we know anything more now than we did?"

"Well, I, for one know lots more." She rubbed her hands over her face, weary. "We are not the same people we were getting into my plane up in Alaska. My endurance has increased, so has yours and Jed's. I was not in bad shape, you were in poor shape, and Jed was in excellent shape, and we are now able to perform at levels that I have never seen before. I can hold my breath for a very long time..." she looked at Jed, who nodded.

"Yes, they ran that test by me, too."

"We know it isn't airborne, by the way," she continued. "the doc told me that after he had us all breathing into those tubes. My guess is that they were looking to see if we were exhaling little critters. It is, however, blood borne."

"What does that mean?" Paul asked.

"It means that, like AIDS, if you bleed on someone, or exchange bodily fluids, they can get our friendly little bug." Jed answered.

"The ultimate parasite," Gabi murmured. "It enhances its host to be sure of its food source."

"Yech." Paul grimaced. "Um, just how much is it 'enhancing' us?"

"I think that is what our doctors are trying to determine." Gabi ran both hands through her hair. "Dibs on the shower."

"Go ahead," the men told her.

After she was in the bathroom, Paul asked Jed "Um, did they take a sample from you....?"

Jed grinned wryly. "Yeah."

"Any idea why?"

"No - probably to determine if the bug can be transferred that way, too."

"Oh." Paul lapsed into thoughtful silence.

After dinner, they retired to their respective bedrooms. Gabi and Jed found a double bed in their room, but without even saying a word, they knew they would not be intimate that night. There were too many watching eyes and listening ears. Instead, Jed held his wife in his arms, and they talked quietly.

"Funny thing, today." Jed began.

"Hmm?" she nuzzled into his shoulder, eyes closed.

"I had a vasectomy seven years ago. But it seems to have been - er - repaired."

"What!" her eyes flew open and she jerked her head back to look at him. "How did you figure that out.... oh."

"I can always have it done again." he said drily.

Her eyes narrowed as she thought. "I don't think it would work. I think the parasite has other ways of guaranteeing its perpetuation. Interesting... I'm going to start calling it a symbiote. More friendly sounding."

"I love the devious way your brain works," he chuckled. "I thought you'd be more upset."

"No, why?"

"Go to sleep." he murmured, not wanting to start an argument. "We'll talk later."

"OK." She was asleep almost immediately, just before he slept as well, although he had wanted to stay awake and think about their situation. But two nights of sleeping on hospital chairs caught up with him, and he fell into exhaustion.

Guinea Pigs

The next morning Dr. Drentz joined them cheerfully for breakfast and updated them on the discoveries they had made thus far. He willingly sat down with them and accepted a plate of food before beginning.

"It is really quite fascinating," he said happily. "Gabrielle, would you like to review...?" he pushed the files at his elbow towards her.

She sighed. "I was wondering if you would recognize me. Yes, I would like to see those."

She bent over the papers, her brow furrowed in thought, as the doctor applied himself to his breakfast. Jed quirked an eyebrow at him, inviting further information.

Drentz explained, "I met her at a conference six years ago, she was presenting a paper. I believe you left the military service shortly after, yes?"

Gabi looked up. "Yes. I Looked a lot different then, so I was curious if you would know me again."

Once again, she returned to her perusal of test results, but her mind was only half with her task. She was remembering the dreadful sequence of

events that had led to her early
retirement from the military. It had
started well enough, if somewhat
challenging, a humanitarian mission to
help an African village in the throes of
a little known disease. That disease is
well enough known now, as one of the most
feared diseases known to man, the Ebola
virus. But then, they had been just
discovering its malignant
characteristics, and she had been ordered
to collect samples and bring them back
with her. Upon her return to her home
base, the labs at USAMRIID, she was
revolted to find that she was wanted to
explore the possibility of using Ebola as
a bioweapon. She had gone to her
commander and protested, then, when there
was no response, chosen to retire early.
She could no longer, after watching the
dreadful events unfolding in a tiny
African village, contemplate developing
weapons designed to kill randomly and
horribly.

With an effort, she refocussed on her
task. The organism the three of them
carried in their blood had definitely
developed from the fine dust contained
within the box. That had been an
encapsulated form of the parasite, and
when inhaled, had quickly revived and
invaded their bloodstream. Once in the
body, however, it behaved like no
parasite she had ever encountered. It was

probably, based on the evidence before her, reprogramming their bodies on the most basic level - improving their DNA and tricking it into re-growing cells at an incredible rate. Not only this, but old injuries, especially in Jed's case, were vanishing, replace by young, strong bone and tissue. The regrowth of his vas deferens in particular interested her, for it was almost as if the parasite - no, symbiote - was ensuring that its host would reproduce. It would, indeed, seem to be the ultimate symbiote. It was enhancing its food source to provide a secure home, lots of food - she had noted the increased metabolism - and the continuation of the species.

"You know," she commented. "I don't think we can continue to call this organism a parasite. By definition, a parasite feeds without giving anything back to the host, but this little beggar seems to be giving us almost as much as it is getting. It is really a symbiote."

"Yes," Doctor Drentz agreed, "I saw that, as well, but until we know for sure that there is not some fatal flaw somewhere, I would like to continue to call it a parasite."

"Ok, but I don't think we will find an ill-effect. This thing is too well designed," she handed the sheaf of paper back to him, her face grim.

He looked shocked. She shook her head at him. "You had to know that I would catch that. No alien pathogen is going to adapt so readily to a human host - certainly not with such excellent effects on our DNA."

He looked chagrined, but only for a moment. "I did see that it had to have been tailored to homo sapiens." he admitted. "But it could not have been done here on Earth."

"Bull puckey." she said bluntly, blue eyes blazing. "What better test group than we are? Jed, magnificent specimen of a soldier, but aging..." Jed bowed ironically. "Myself, with the know-how to tell you exactly what is happening to us - because I know it myself - and Paul..." she paused, looking Dr. Drentz in the eye. "Paul, who was diabetic, and is no longer."

Paul sat up very straight with a muffled exclamation.

"Charles," she continued, "Tell me the truth, please, do not play with me!"

He shrugged, eyes sparkling. Her scolding had not daunted him a bit.

"I wish we could have created this organism, my dear colleague. But the truth is that as far as genetic research has come these past few years, we are still generations away from producing anything with even part of this - this.... symbiote's capabilities. Have you thought the results through? Do you see, as I do, that the effects and progress of aging has likely come to a virtual stop, and in some areas has actually been reversed? It is beyond comprehension! I cannot even begin to tell you how it was done, only that it was... and what the consequence will be I do not know."

"A methuselah germ." muttered Paul, still shocky from the discovery that his disease was gone.

Charles Drentz shot him a piercing glance. "Yes, I think that is a very accurate name for it, Mr. Monroe...

"Paul, please." Paul said.

"Paul. I project that all of you will have greatly extended life spans if the symbiote stays with you. This is indeed the germ of a new thing. The beginning."

Gabi, who had not yet thought of this aspect, sat back, eyes narrowed in thought. Jed and Paul sat silently, stunned by the suddenness of the change in themselves, trying to comprehend what it meant to them. That they were now more than they had been, because of a minute bug - a bug! - in their blood was perturbing.

"Just the three of us." said Gabi a minute later. "We are carriers of something that may well be capable of healing and extending the life of a man...."

She sat back, burdened by the enormity of it. "What happened to the dust?"

Doctor Drentz shook his head, regretfully. "We had small samples off your clothes, but the clothing was incinerated. Perhaps the plane..." he shrugged.

"Why would something out there..." she gestured at the ceiling "The Others, for lack of a better term."

"Aliens?" muttered Jed with a sly grin.

She ignored him, "Why would they do this to us? What is the purpose in infecting us with an organism that strengthens us and prolongs our life?"

"I don't know, but if you will assist me, I would like to study the organism itself to try to discover more not only about it, but its makers."

"Of course," she nodded, "thank you for inviting me."

Dangers and Delays

"Come look, Gabrielle."

"Just a minute." she stretched stiff muscles as she looked up from her microscope. "Two weeks. Two weeks we've been at this, and what do we know? No more than we guessed at the beginning!"

Gabi reached Dr. Drentz's side and asked, "What am I looking at?"

"We do know more," he reproved, indicating the culture dish he was working on to her. "We have proven that you three are carrying a highly sophisticated symbiote, designed to inhabit _homo sapiens_. One that is capable of genetic manipulation...."

"Good Lord!" she interrupted him. "Is this really Paul's blood?"

"Yes, although it could be any one of you."

"It is exhibiting the characteristics of stem cells... it is actually encouraging these cells to divide. Fascinating...."

"It is not rampant, however," he rubbed his nose. "That would lead to a cancer like condition. The parasites only do this when prompted, as at the site of an injury. I cultured this from samples taken at the site of Paul's leg wound."

"So we have our own built in swift-heal. Well, nice to have that confirmed. Charles, what are you going to do about us?"

He turned away from her and walked toward the door, pulling off his gloves.

"You can't avoid this," she said.

She followed him down the ugly green corridor, with its ducts looming overhead and oppressing her. She wished the army would consider the mental health and well-being of its personnel just once while designing a building. She wished Charles would stop and talk to her. She had seen him changing over the last two days from the cheerful man they had met on their arrival, to a morose and brooding doctor who was becoming ever more detached from her. Finally, she stopped dead and stamped her foot.

Dr. Drentz turned and looked back at her, startled by this uncharacteristic display.

"Good. Now that I have your attention, would it inconvenience you to tell me what is going on?"

Sighing, he said, "If you will accompany me to your rooms. I only want to say this once."

"All right. Now, why couldn't you just tell me that?"

"I have been, as you guessed, struggling with a dilemma."

"And?"

"I have made a decision."

At the door to their hastily furnished suite of rooms, he stopped and chivalrously allowed her to proceed him through the door. Inside, he picked up the phone and made a couple of phone calls. Gabi busied herself with fussing over their scavenged coffeepot, coaxing it to produce enough coffee for everyone she knew would be showing up shortly.

Jed and Paul showed up shortly, both damp from the shower. She guessed that they had been in the gym. Jed had been bored and purposeless until he figured out what to do - teach Paul what to do with his newly enhanced muscles. The two of them had been working their way through a miniature version of ranger school ever since, with quite a lot of macho glee at their new prowess. She knew - they gloated over it every night.

"Anything wrong?" Jed searched her face.

"No nasties showing up in the blood?" Paul grinned. He was adjusting to his new self by producing new personality, as far as she could tell. Once quiet and reserved, he was now a joker and wiseacre.

"Colonel Matthewson." She nodded at the next arrival. He smiled at her, seeming to enjoy the sight of her as much as he had said at their first meeting, when he told her with a grin that she was

the missing link. In what? she had asked.
In understanding Jed, he had told her
quite seriously, in understanding why his
junior was a driven man, but seemingly
without an aim.

"No, dear, nothing wrong with us."
she tilted her head slightly back for
Jed's gentle kiss. "Doctor D needed a
conference."

When they were all seated around the
table - filched from the dining facility,
she had no doubt - Dr. Drentz cleared his
throat.

"Colonel Matthewson, thank you for
coming. To begin, I want to sum up for
you what Dr. McGregor and I have
discovered, or confirmed."

He continued for several moments,
stopping only to explain technicalities
to the Colonel's occasional query. Gabi
appreciated that the Colonel was humble
enough to ask, she had known too many
stuffed shirts who would have just sat
there and nodded, then gone off without
understanding a thing.

When he was finished, the colonel
leaned back in his chair, lacing fingers
over his slight paunch.

"So what these three are are carriers
of a symbiotic organism that enhances its
host to be capable of darn near anything,
and heals very rapidly any injury that
host may sustain, and also ensures that
that host will reproduce?"

"Yes." Dr. Drentz nodded emphatically, pleased at the comprehension.

"Well now, this is a problem."

"Why?" asked Gabi.

"I can think of all kinds of things." Jed broke in. "All kinds of uses that could be found for us - or at least, for our friendly little bugs."

"Two days ago, I had to inform Dr. David Lewiston of what was happening." Dr. Drentz continued, looking uncomfortable.

Gabi gasped and sat upright. Jed looked grim. Paul looked at both of them and quizzically back at the doctor.

"What is wrong, Dr. McGregor?" the Colonel asked.

"My former boss. The reason I left the army. The reason _I_ don't call myself a doctor any longer. Coming here, I suppose?" she directed the last at Dr. Drentz.

He nodded. "He is due in tomorrow morning."

"Well, then." Gabi stood abruptly and said, "Excuse me, gentlemen." and walked into the bedroom she shared with Jed and closed the door firmly. She did not slam it, but the sound of its closing was enough to deter anyone from following her.

Jed sighed and looked at the faces of the men around him. They mirrored their feelings - concern, mostly.

"She did not part on good terms with him. The man is a pig."

"I had to, Captain. I am sorry, but it is my duty to report my findings to my superior."

"I know, Dr. D. Don't apologize. She knows it too. So, what happens next?"

Consequences

"To satisfy you, I will add myself, or if he wishes, Dr. Drentz."

Dr. Lewiston looked down his lengthy nose at Gabi, smiling in such a way that made her shiver. She knew he was manipulating her, and she felt helpless.

Inwardly raging at the complete reversion to their roles all those years ago, she said, "I still maintain that conducting trials on humans in such a hasty manner in not only of dubious use, but unethical. What do you hope to accomplish?"

"Why do you persist in assuming I wish to be hasty? I only want to determine if, and how, your symbiote can be transferred." he raised an eyebrow. "I am sure you have wondered that yourself. Don't you want to find out the answer?"

"Yes, but I am not yet sure there will be no ill effects."

"Well, there have been none so far in your case, or in Captain McGregor, or Mr. Monroe. And as your own research has already shown, we cannot test the organism in any other species. It requires _homo sapiens_ as its host."

She ground her teeth. He was spinning everything around to his way, and she would have given anything to know what he wanted. She knew he wanted something, she had never seen him do anything without personal gain.

"Very well."

"Excellent," he favored her with a toothy smile. "Shall we begin tomorrow?"

She turned on her heel and stalked out of the lab, away from the slimy bastard.

Which was exactly what she called him a few moments later, talking to Jed. He laughed.

"Obscenity, from you? He still has that way about him, I take it?"

"Yes. Oh, I could just..." she fluttered her hands, speechless.

"Easy, darling." He wrapped his arms around her and she leaned into him, eyes suddenly filling with tears.

"Oh, Jed, how have I gotten on without you?"

"Hmmm?" his voice was muffled in her hair. She pressed her cheek closer to his chest the better to hear his heart beat

"All these years, wasted, because I was afraid. I am so sorry."

She lifted her head, and he gazed into her tear-wet eyes. "Never apologize. I wasn't easy to live with, and I certainly didn't give in any, either. But that is the past, and we are here, now, and have a chance to go on. More of a chance than we may yet realize."

She could see that he had been thinking about the likelihood that they would have very elongated life spans. So had she, and it was overwhelming her to think that not only did she have a second chance with him, but a second chance to have a family.

"Jed, what do you think about us having children?"

"Gabrielle." He leaned his forehead against hers. "There is so much more to consider in that now. So much we don't know. You know I would love to watch you carrying our child... but what about our friendly little bugs?"

"What about them? Jed, I think they are designed to reproduce right along with us."

"Maybe, but Gabi, I am not sure I am willing to use our child as an experiment."

"What is any child but an experiment?"

He linked his hands around her slender waist and held her loosely in the circle of his arms. She stood quietly, trusting him.

"I want you to have our children," he said slowly. "I think we would make beautiful babies together..." he favored her with his Groucho Marx leer, which made her giggle. "But I think we need to find out more about the symbiote. And,

Gabi, I almost lost you. I want to have you all to myself for a while."

She nodded, brushing the tears from her cheeks. "You are right. I don't know what I was thinking."

Jed frowned. "Gabi, have you considered that the symbiote might be sentient? That would explain its rapid adaptation to our system, and your sudden compulsion to have children..."

She clapped a hand to her mouth and knew her eyes widened at this horrifying thought. If the Others who designed the symbiote were, in fact, inside them...

"I have to see Dr. D." she said. "Thank you!" she called over her shoulder, already out of the room, lab coat streaming behind her as she strode down the corridor.

"Charles," she called upon entering the lab. "Have you thought that there is the possibility..."

She broke off, seeing Dr. Lewiston. She stopped and closed up her emotions, knowing he could see her face lose expression, and not caring. He was no longer her boss, and had no real power over her.

"David," she nodded cooly at him. She wouldn't do him the dignity of calling him a doctor.

"What is wrong, Gabrielle?" Charles asked.

"Had you considered the possibility of sentience?"

"No, not really," he considered. "I don't think so. They seem to be using the same patterns and cycles constantly - I haven't seen any behavior changes triggered by situation."

"We need to be sure, though. I do not wish to be a puppet wielded by something inside me."

He nodded. "How would we test that though?"

"Well, if the symbiote really can think... and wants to preserve its host at all costs. I think it may have been giving me a mental compulsion earlier - anyway I said something I hadn't intended to."

David Lewiston, listening with interest, chuckled. "We all do that, Doctor McGregor."

"Yes, I realize that, but it occurred to Jed that we may have made an assumption in thinking the symbiote was designed. It would be simpler to assume that it adapted to us because it _wanted_ to."

"So what you were thinking of as a test was to offer harm to one of you and see if the symbiote takes over?" Charles asked.

She nodded, "Yes."

"Hmmm..." He turned away, lost in thought.

"There is a hole in your reasoning," David Lewiston informed her. "If it were sentient and not designed specifically for humans, it would accept other species as host, simply for its own survival in the absence of a human."

"It may do that anyway. May I remind you that we do not know its entire life cycle yet. It is entirely likely that while it spends one phase of life in our bodies - adulthood, say - it needs another host species to spend the larval stage in. There are terrestrial species that live in just that way."

He inclined his head. "I bow to your expertise, my dear."

Her eyes glittered dangerously at his cynical tone. "Then cancel the human trial until we find out the answer to this. You do not know what you may be inflicting on innocent people."

He shook his head, smiling. "Nice try, but this is too big for you to stop. With the capabilities this symbiote gives to a man, the - ahem - life cycle is of little importance. Any tradeoff will be worth it to be enhanced as you are." He straightened from the counter he had been leaning his hip against, and strolled from the room. Gabi stared after him, fuming. He was willing to trade off the health and safety of twelve people for the possibility that they would be supermen.

Charles came up behind her. "Your fists are clenched, Gabrielle." he pointed out with gentle amusement in his voice.

She laughed shortly. "He infuriates me. Charles, do you think there is any way of killing off the symbiote in our blood?"

He twisted his lips in thought. "Probably... Oh. You just may have proved that the symbiote does not control your brain."

"What?"

"Two things. One, you would be all over this experiment if all you were concerned about was the propagation of yourself - that is, the symbiote. Two, you would not be able to suggest so calmly killing all your friendly inhabitants off."

She sighed in relief, and he grinned at her. "That is a weight off my mind. I hated the idea of being controlled."

"Now, about the trial." she continued. "How are you planning to conduct it?"

"I had thought to centrifuge the organism out of your blood - I have already taken blood from Jed to do so."

"Why Jed?"

"He is military, and I did not have to have his consent. I did not think you would give me yours, or that Paul would agree either."

"It hadn't occurred to me to say no." she admitted. "But I don't like the idea of the military having so much control over Jed's body."

"Then I had planned on injecting it directly into our bloodstreams."

She met his eyes. "You are taking part?"

"Yes." he said steadily. "I do not think there will be much danger - none of the three of you suffered any ill effects at all. Oh, yes, could you please go over for me again what you did feel."

"Well, we inhaled the encapsulated form, remember. It must have hatched in mucous membranes and crossed through to the bloodstream. Given the rapidity of our healing, I would have to say it reproduced very quickly and did not arouse the alarm in our immune system." She shrugged. "As for the rest, I was comatose for much of the first forty-eight hours. Paul and Jed reported excessive sleepiness, and ravenous hunger. I think the symbiote must pull from existing resources to accelerate replication of itself ..."

He looked thoughtful. They knew the organism was reproducing asexually, dividing itself asunder over and over. When it reached a certain level in the blood, it stopped reproducing, and both she and Charles thought that this would trigger a start to a sexual reproduction cycle.

"We need to devise a test against allergic reactions."

"Yes," he nodded. "I had already thought of that. I will heat up and kill a batch of the organism and then scratch test."

"Good," she began to pace, head down. "That was what I was most worried about, a sudden catastrophic allergic reaction. There is no need to lose anyone to anaphylactic shock. Also, some may have immune systems that will fend it off. They may spike a fever in doing so. And is it conceivable this thing will mutate on us? We don't need to have anyone dissolving into their component parts."

"A puddle of unlinked DNA on the floor?"

She laughed at his dry tone and amused look. "Ok, I am overreacting."

He laughed with her. "Gabi, I think we have covered all the bases. Why don't you go get some food and rest?"

"One good thing about our little friend," she remarked, "I never forget a meal anymore. At one time I could go all day without remembering food."

"Go on," he shooed her out of the lab.

As she walked along the bleak corridor she thought about her husband and his military service. She did not like the way David Lewiston had taken his blood without so much as a by-your-leave. She pursed her lips in thought and headed for Colonel Matthewson's room. He answered her knock with "Enter."

She went in and saw him sitting at the tiny desk, working with a mountain of paperwork. "Sorry to disturb, you, sir."

He stood up, smiling. "Not at all, Dr. McGregor. It is a pleasure to escape this for a moment." He pulled the chair around and motioned for her to sit. "Please, call me Gabi," she asked.

"Well, then, Gabi, what can I do for you?"

"It's about Jed." He nodded understanding. "I don't like that he is available as Dr. Lewiston's personal guinea pig."

"You know, when Jed met me when I came in, he mentioned that he has only a month left until re-up. He could take early retirement, you know."

She shook her head. "That is not my decision to make. I came because he respects you, and I think you are a decent man. Can you somehow remove him from this mess?"

He sat silently for a moment, evidently lost in thought. Then he looked up at her. "Well, I am mighty curious about the change in that meteor's direction. There was nothing about the specimen you brought in to indicate a reason for that. I think Jed didn't finish a job up there." his eyes twinkled, and she grinned back.

"Rangers don't quit, even on a rock-retrieval mission?"

"Yep." he continued, mischief in his eyes, "And you are going to have to go home soon - this project can't last forever."

"Sir, for an Army man, you are a decent fellow," she deadpanned.

He laughed. "I'll take that as a compliment."

Arguments

Jed was seeing red that evening as he strode into their rooms. "Excuse us, Paul," he said curtly, taking Gabi's elbow and steering her to their bedroom. She protested, but he steeled himself against her, and shut the door behind them.

"What the hell did you think you were doing?" he demanded in a low voice.

"What?"

"I can take care of the situation without you protecting me. I gave my blood to Lewiston because I knew he'd get it somehow, and I didn't want him harassing you, or Paul. But you go to Colonel Matt and have me sent off on some wild goose chase... Gabi, I won't have it!"

"I didn't ask anything of the colonel. All I did was tell him my concerns. I know you are a proud soldier - but I am your wife and I hate the idea of you being Lewiston's guinea pig!"

"You haven't been that concerned these last six years." he said coldly, then regretted it when he heard her gasp of pain

"Yes, I was. Why do you think I left the military?" She blinked back the tears. "I couldn't bear to think of you being in the front line of some attack, exposed to some vile disease I helped create!"

"I am a warrior." he ground out. "You have always known that. When the call comes, I go. It is as much a part of me as my love for you. But this was unnecessary. I need to be _here_." He threw out his hands in disgust, and she flinched. Startled, he stared at her a minute, then felt the blood leave his face. She had thought he would hit her.

"Gabi, I would never strike you." he said in a shaky but gentle tone. "Oh, god, I frightened you."

"No, no, it's silly. I know you wouldn't hit me... just old habit."

"I forgot. God forgive me, I forgot what that evil bastard did to you."

She touched his arm. He stood stock still, trying to look harmless. Her former boyfriend had beaten her, once. Jed had found her trying to fight the man off with a broken arm dangling at her side, screaming like a berserker. Jed hadn't known her then, but it made his blood boil to see the valiant fight she was putting up against a man twice her size. He had waded right in alongside her and beat the man until she was clutching Jed's arm and telling him to stop. Jed had stood up, panting, and she had walked closer to her assailant and looked at him with iron in her gaze. "You deserve to die," she had said, "But I'll not have this brave soldier suffer because if it." Then she had simply walked away. Jed thought he had fallen in love then and there, with the first woman he had met who was his match. Now his heart was pounding in his chest. Of all the stupid things for him to do... he had never even raised his voice to her before, and now he had to do this.

"Jed." she put her hands on his chest, looking up into his eyes. All traces of anger were gone from them. "Jed, I love you and I trust you. I know you will not strike me. It is just a reflex."

Heavily, he sat down on the bed and pulled her into his lap. "Sorry, so sorry," he said, burying his face in her hair and smelling her sweet scent. "I'm being macho, not wanting to leave you alone here with that man. I hated what he did to you before. I don't want to see you become that wilted little flower you were before."

"I put too much stock in what he said, before. He was supposed to be my mentor, and I gave him too much power. I'll not make that mistake again. Besides," she teased gently "I have the symbiote. He can't possibly touch me or I'll tear his arm off."

Jed tightened his arms around her. "Valkyrie." he growled with a smile.

"Heh. Want to see what this valkyrie can do?" she asked, pushing him backwards onto the bed.

"Hey! you realize they are probably watching?"

"I don't care."

In the morning, Jed told Paul that he was going back up to Alaska to see if they had missed part of the meteor.

Paul asked "Do you need a geologist?"

Jed shook his head. "Not right away. But I may later. When you come up, you might keep Gabi company."

Jed saw that Paul caught on quickly, and after a flickered glance at Gabi, who was demurely eating her breakfast, he said "Sure, pretty company will never be turned down by me."

Jed coughed, laughing inside at the young man's teasing. Gabi caught his eye and they grinned at one another. He stood, knowing he had to go, and she walked him to the door. "I'll miss you. It's hard, now that I've decided I was stupid to let you go for so long." she said.

He kissed her gently. "I will be waiting for you." he promised, hugging her close. Then he turned and walked away, feeling wrenched by his desire to be near her, and his orders.

Testing, Testing...

Gabi stared after his retreating back, her vision blurred by tears.

Paul asked brightly from behind her, "So what's on the agenda for today?"

She turned and blinked back the tears. Smiling to show her appreciation at his attempt to distract her, she replied "That human trial. We are injecting twelve people with the bug today."

Paul sat alone in the room, reading, for quite awhile after she had gone. He was jerked out of the daydream he was indulging in when the phone rang. He picked it up.

"Paul, get to the lab now. I need you," said Gabi, and hung up.

Gabi met a breathless Paul at the door. "Here, put these on," she said abruptly, shoving a mask and gloves into his hands. He followed her, fumbling with them into another room, where twelve people were lying or sitting on beds. There were two orderlies moving through the room. Gabi began to explain as she went from person to person, conducting a quick examination on each one.

"We started with the allergy test, eliminated two that way, then injected the rest, and right away something went wrong.... Damn!" she swore, bending over the man in the second bed, feeling for a pulse. "He's gone."

W-what ?" stammered Paul.

"Their systems are rejecting it," she said grimly. They are spiking fevers of 107, going into convulsions... and some of them are dying."

"Here," she shoved a five-gallon bucket of ice and water into his hands. "We have to get his fever down, and I am not taking the risk of communicating it to anyone else. Joe and Carlos have volunteered, against my advice, but they are good fellows." She looked rather fondly at the other two men, bent over patients administering ice to their extremities.

"Don't put ice on his torso," she warned. "I don't want to shock his heart. It is already working overtime."

She continued down the line, leaving him with the third patient. He started to put ice around the man's arms and legs to replace the ice already melting there. Gabi returned with a cloth. "Sponge down his body, please," as she turned away, she squeezed Paul's arm. "Thank you."

Paul didn't pay too much attention to what was going on around him, merely drizzling the prone form before him with ice water and replacing the ice frequently. Gabi checked on him occasionally, and he was distantly aware that she was doing the same thing as he. It seemed like an interminable time before Gabi stopped his arm. "Enough, Paul. His fever has broken."

Paul stepped back and looked around him. The room was a disaster, water and wet cloths everywhere. One of the orderlies was still attending to a patient, but the other was sitting on the floor, leaning his head back against the wall. Gabi bent over him and took his shoulder. "You ok, Carlos?"

"Yes, ma'am," the man muttered wearily. "I lost him."

"I know," she said sympathetically.

She checked the last patient and sighed. "His temp is down two points. Keep it up a while longer, Joe."

"Yes ma'am."

Paul marveled at her poise in the midst of the chaos. She came back to stand before him and he saw the pain in her eyes. "We lost five." she said "And I think that six of the rest may have brain damage - they were the ones with the highest fevers for the longest time. In particular Dr. Lewiston. Joe's working on him. One of them went to sleep - or a coma, not sure yet."

As she spoke, the man on the end of the row of beds sat up and gasped audibly. "My god, Gabrielle! What happened?"

"Charles! Oh, thank God!" she looked as though she would like to kiss him as she hurried to his side, Paul following. "It was a disaster."

Consequences

She filled him in quickly. He was pale and shaking, but looked otherwise healthy. Gabi realized what was wrong and sent Carlos after food for her colleague. He tore into it when it was put before him, and gradually regained color. When he was finished, Gabi, who had been moving about the room issuing low-voiced orders and assisting with the changing of bed-linens, returned to his side and sat down near the foot of the bed.

"Well, how do you feel?"

"Good, except there seems to be something wrong with my eyes. You don't thin it could be encysting there...?" he asked with some alarm, thinking of a particularly nasty terrestrial parasite that did just that.

She shook her head, chuckling. "Try taking your glasses off."

"Oh." Then, as he removed them, "Oh!"

She smiled slightly, "Welcome to a very exclusive little club, Charles. I think you are the fourth human to contract the methuselah germ."

"Just me?"

She nodded. "I don't think any of the others... I'll wait for blood tests, of course, but I think they would either have re-acted the way you did - by falling asleep - or be healing already, and that isn't happening."

"Damn."

She sighed. "Yes. That fool. That poor fool."

Did he make it?"

"Yes, barely. I don't think there is much left of his brain. Cooked oatmeal," she finished grimly. "I despised the man, but no one deserves that."

Just then, Joe called her. She went to Dr. Lewiston's bedside and bent over him for a few minutes. Then she came back to Charles with an expression of incredulity on her face. "He's recovering."

Paul, who had been sitting on the now empty bed next to the doctor's, looked up in surprise. "I thought he was the worst."

She shrugged. "Sometimes the human body is a strange thing. Throw the symbiote into the mix, and who knows?"

Charles yawned widely. "I'm sleepy again." he said in surprise.

"Get some sleep. Paul, you too. I'll get some as soon as I finish up here."

Paul nodded, and staggered to his feet. He yawned, and Gabi waved him out of the room with a smile. Her face grew more serious as she turned back to her patients. The bodies had been removed, and there were empty beds scattered through the room. She noted their placement, confirming their randomness. She hadn't thought there would be a pattern, but it was a well-trained habit to look for any connection, any clue. Her past as an epidemiologist had been a lot of detective work. She made her way through the room, checking each one and soothing occasionally with her ungloved hands. She noted that the restless patients calmed at her touch. She enjoyed the rare privilege of human contact with her patients. She was not worried about catching anything from them. They had been pretty well screened, and she had a good idea that her symbiote would ward off intruders. She paused by Dr. Lewiston's bedside and felt his forehead, then, more scientifically, took his temperature. It was down to normal, she noted with approval, but she did not like his pallor. She ordered an i.v. for him and came back to Charles, who was sound asleep, snoring slightly. She smiled down at him, greeted the next shift of nurses who would watch her patients through the night, and left orders to be awakened at any changes. Then she wearily trudged back to her room and fell on the bed fully clothed, asleep before she hit the bed.

Answer Quest

Jed leaned his head back and closed his eyes, pretending to be asleep. He couldn't sleep, his mind was in such a turmoil, but he thought it best to project his usual facade of tough-guy unconcern. He had never before considered disobeying an order, but he had almost told Colonel Matthewson to shove it. He hated leaving Gabi alone - well, almost alone, but Paul didn't really count - and going off on some wild goose chase. Jed told himself that she knew he was a soldier, she had manifestly known it since the moment she met him, but it still gnawed at him that he had just abandoned his wife. Six years before, he had chosen his career and the military over her, but now, he realized, he would not do that again. She deserved all of him, not just what the military left behind. He smiled, seeing her in his mind's eye as he had seen her so recently in Alaska. That was her home, her place. She had looked so natural and confident there, such a far cry from the pale woman who had almost subverted her entire self to the military - and to him, he realized now.

Once he had made his decision, he relaxed. Drifting happily in thoughts of sharing a home with Gabi and using his skills to make a living as a back-country guide, Jed fell asleep. Ever a light sleeper, he snapped awake when the plane touched down and silently began a mental inventory of what he would need to set out into the wilderness again. He would need shelter - a warm sleeping bag would be a must, as they entered the short fall season, nights were quite chilly. Food, a filtration system so he could drink the water... Focused on his mission now, he snapped a salute at the sergeant waiting for him, and followed him.

He was escorted to a helicopter, and shown his gear already onboard.

"We're going to drop you off right where the brush fire started." the pilot told him. "What are you looking for?"

"I don't know." Jed said truthfully, thinking that he didn't really want to find anything.

Patently not believing him, the pilot shrugged and said "Hop in."

Jed rather enjoyed the ride out. Endless dark green forest unrolled below them. In the valleys he could see the muskeg, swathed in the brilliant scarlet of its fall foliage. Every so often he glimpsed the silver thread of a stream or a river, flanked by the flaming gold of aspen and birch. They swooped over the sluggish brown of the Tanana river, and the copilot remarked over the intercom,

"Locals say there is so much suspended silt and rock in that river that a body dropped in there will disappear forever. They swear it's been done, too."

The sun was beginning to set when they reached their destination, and the soft peach color playing over the snowcapped Alaska range took his breath away. The pilot, glancing out at the spectacle, commented, "Mountain Fire, they call that. Hope you have a good stay."

Jed gave him a thumbs-up, shoving his gear out the open door before jumping out himself. The chopper rose up and circled once, then made a beeline back for the base, waved on by Jed. He stood still for a moment, watching the silhouette of the helicopter disappear into the brilliant colors of the sunset, then quickly set up camp. He chose an un-scorched area under the trees, pleased to feel the deep moss as he knelt to erect his tent. The moss was sprinkled with little plants that had rounded, glossy leaves and bright maroon berries. He recognized these as lingonberries, and picked a double handful of them. Finished with his camp, he hunted around for rock and made a fireplace. With the deep moss and duff, he decided to put his fire out on the edge of the scorched area, lest he start another forest fire. By the time he had a few cheerful flames leaping in his

impromptu fire-ring, the stars were out.
He walked a little way out into the
artificial clearing left by the fire,
looking up. The sky overhead was vast,
dusted with silver stars. He had not
often seen the sky like this. He could
remember a few times, on missions to out-
of-the way places in the world, but
usually he had been too busy, too tense,
or just too downright scared to pay much
attention. Tonight he was in no hurry,
and he just turned his face to the sky
and marveled.

When he turned back to his little
fire, someone was sitting next to it. Jed
stopped breathing for a moment, scanning
for others, or any danger he could
detect, but the night was as still about
him as it had been a minute ago. He could
see nothing, feel nothing... but there
was someone sitting there, back to him,
evidently watching the flames. As he drew
nearer, walking very quietly, he could
smell the berries he had left in his
canteen cup cooking. It was a tart, spicy
scent that teased at him, until suddenly
he remembered that he had not yet put
them on to cook when he stepped away.

He was only a pace or two from the
figure bent over his fire when it turned
and slid the cowl back and off its head.
He stopped again, knowing only one thing
in that instant. The Others had found
him. It - she? - was beautiful,

shimmering in the firelight. She looked astonishingly human, he realized. He couldn't help thinking of her as female. She was cloaked from head to toe in a brown, soft-looking material. Her head and face were all that he could really see, but the outline beneath her covering was right for two arms and two legs. Her face... she had a nose, mouth, and eyes, but no hair. Her skin was transparent, except for her delicately pink lips, and he could see the tracery of blue veins beneath it. Her skin was also iridescent. It shimmered and glowed in the firelight. He wondered at his reaction to her. She seemed beautiful, but so alien, yet he could not shake the feeling of overwhelming recognition of her beauty.

Her lips curved in a slight smile. "Welcome."

He blinked. She spoke perfect English. Her voice was very high, and he thought it sounded like bells ringing. "Hello." he managed, feeling rather foolish.

"You admire beauty." she said, turning back to the fire and stirring the cooking berries.

"Uh, yes." he sat down across from her, wondering if she meant herself, or his stargazing.

"I added a little sugar to them."

"Good, they are too tart by themselves." he passed a hand over his eyes, wondering if he was hallucinating.

She seemed to guess what he was thinking and smiled again. "I am not a dream. My name is A'lita, and I think you came back here to find me."

"If you are the um, representative of the race responsible for the symbiote spores in that meteor, yes, I did come here looking for you."

She laughed, and this time he could have sworn he heard bells ringing. He also realized when she opened her mouth that she had no teeth, but a long, tightly curled tongue. "Oh, I am notof them, but our people feel kindly toward yours. I was chosen to meet you, as I am one of the few who can speak your language."

"Um, excuse me, but what are you?"

She had set aside the berries to cool, and now she picked them up and stirred them again, looking rather dubiously at them. "Are you certain these are edible?"

"Well, I know I can eat them without harm. I don't know whether you can."

She shrugged - at least, her cloak rippled - and offered some to him. "I can but try." she said.

He watched, fascinated, as she protruded her tongue and curled it into a straw shape. Delicately, she sipped at the berry mixture. As they had cooked, they had mashed up until they resembled a thin cranberry sauce. She looked back up at him, neatly withdrawing her tongue, and beamed.

"Delicious!"

He chuckled. He couldn't help it, she was so eagerly childlike in her approval.

"Forgive me," she said now. "I did not answer your question before. Our race is called the Orion'ess. We live... " she waved her hand at the sky, and he realized something. She had a very small hand, with only three long fingers and a short thumb. Further, she had no wrist, but an intricately folding system of bone and membrane that half-expanded as she gestured.

"We guessed as much." He said, fascinated and trying to decide just what she was hiding beneath that cloak. "How is it you can speak my language?"

"Oh, we have been studying you for a very long time. At least two generations, and our life spans are double yours." she said earnestly. "But there are very few of us who can master human languages. It takes a great deal of tongue control. See?"

And she opened her mouth and showed him how she was holding her long tongue coiled to approximate the shape of a human tongue. He also saw that although she had no teeth, her gums were bony and

obviously very hard. He realized
something else with this ingenuous
outpouring.

"How old are you, A'Lita?" he had a
problem with the grace note in her name,
but she smiled at his attempt, so he
figured he had gotten close.

"I am 18 of our years. I think..."
she put out the tip of her tongue,
obviously thinking. "That is like 9, or
maybe 10, of yours. Like a child." she
beamed at him again.

He wasn't sure how close that
estimate really was, since she seemed
more advanced to him than a human ten-
year old, but he did think that she was
immature. Unless the whole race was like
this... his mind boggled. No, whoever had
developed the symbiote had known what
they were doing.

"A'Lita? Do you think I could meet
some of the others?"

She smiled. "Soon. They are still
waiting for something." she stopped,
listening, and he realized she was being
spoken to through some unseen
transmitter, and she had a subvocal
portion at her throat, for she touched
her throat and he could see her muscles
move, but no sound. As a soldier, he
approved of the silent method of
communication, and wondered if it was
technology, or part of the Orion'ess
physiology.

She addressed him now. "I must go back. May I come again in the morning?"

"Certainly." he told her gravely, and rose when she did, courteously. She moved stiffly, seeming unused to walking, but the cloak covered her and he still had no idea what she really looked like. She hooded herself and walked away into the darkness, toward the fire scorched areas. He looked after her for a moment, but she had disappeared into the night.

In the morning, as he woke, he wondered if it had been a dream. It had been such a simple, calm encounter. I just made first contact with an alien race, he thought, awed, and all I could think about was whether she would burn her tongue. Then he grabbed the little notebook out of his fatigue blouse and made some notes. He had been so flustered the night before he had not asked the questions that now rushed to mind. He didn't mean to come to his second meeting unprepared. He lay on his back for a moment, staring up at the roof of the low tent and rubbing his jaw in thought. The stubble beneath his fingers made him grimace. He needed to shave. Some representative of the human race he must be, coming to meet the Orion'ess bristly and unwashed. He sighed. There was nothing he could do about the unwashed, but at least he could shave. He wiggled out of the tent and pulled on his boots.

There was a stream not too far away, and he wanted some water.

He was coming back to his camp after a quick dry shave and splash in the stream when he saw her, once again sitting near the fire ring. He swore under his breath. He had hoped for a little more time. He was only wearing his boots and pants, as he had hoped to dry off before he put his shirt back on. A'lita turned and smiled at him. She did not seem to notice his partial undress, and he hoped nudity was not a taboo to her race. Quickly, he pulled his t-shirt over his head, stuffing it into his waistband.

"Good morning," he greeted her.

"Good morning," she returned. "Are you ready to go meet the elders?"

"Uh," he ran his hand over his still damp hair, thankful it was so short. He pulled on his blouse and buttoned it. He debated about taking the pistol he wore at his waist with him, and decided against it. "Just a minute."

He ducked into the tent, kneeling, and stripped off the pistol belt. When he came back out, she was standing and waiting for him. "Ok, I am ready now," he fibbed. He wasn't ready. He desperately wished for a set of full dress greens, a senior level statesman, anybody but him, in his fatigues, to meet these people. He would have happily faced a known enemy

with guns blazing - he had done that -
rather than do this. He was not a
diplomat, for God's sake, he was a
soldier!

His face did not betray his inner
turmoil as he followed A'Lita out into
the fire waste. He marched along calmly
and with all the poise he could muster.
She stopped suddenly and he stood beside
her, wondering, when the air rippled and
an aircraft appeared before them. Jed's
eyes widened, but he recognized the
technology behind what he had just seen.
Granted, he had never seen anything
approaching the sophistication of it, but
it was not totally alien. The craft
itself was shaped rather like a squid
without the tentacles. It was sleek,
slim, and rather deadly looking. He
admired the shape of it, and the beauty.
A ramp extended from the middle, just
behind the flaring openings of what he
guessed was its propulsion system. A'lita
led him to this, and they were met by two
other Orion'ess. They were taller than
A'lita, and, like her, cloaked. The male,
distinguished by his heavier, more
defined features and slightly larger
frame, wore a dull blue cloak. The
female, who looked remarkably like
A'lita, wore a crimson cloak. They both
smiled at him and bowed slightly. Jed,
feeling rather foolish, bowed back. When
he straightened they were beaming at him.

The two exchanged a glance, then the female spoke to A'lita. Her voice was very high and carrying, with that sound of bells he had noted in A'lita.

A'Lita translated. "Mother is very impressed."

The male spoke now, his speech carrying a definite flavor of amusement.

"Oh, I am sorry. I need to introduce them," she looked flustered for the first time that he had seen. "My father, A'fri, and my mother, A'lina. They are the first ambassadors to Earth," she finished rather proudly.

He was surprised, "And they are meeting with me?"

"Yes," A'lita translated. "They had counted on your curiosity to bring you back here, and they did not want to alarm humanity by approaching something like the UN or the White House first, without warning."

He noted that they were addressing him directly, although A'lita spoke the English words for them. He rather liked that, and talked back directly to them. "Probably wise, at that. But why me?"

"We did not choose you, you came to us. Won't you come in?"

He threw caution to the wind and said, "Yes, I'd like that, thank you."

The interior was hushed, but beautiful. The walls were pastel colors that changed as he proceeded into the craft. They took him into a small room with a table in the center and chairs around it. Once seated, A'fri began.

"I have no doubt that you have many questions," Jed thought of the list of them in his pocket. "But please let me begin with a little history. About two hundred of your years ago, the Orion'ess came across your planet. We had been surveying this arm of your galaxy for quite some time, and we were surprised and pleased to find it inhabited. We set up a listening post and went on our way, content to merely observe and not interfere with your culture. We did not learn much about you until recently, with the advent of satellites that we could tap into, and the internet. But by then we had a post on the planet, and this is why."

A'fri pulled out an object that looked, to Jed's eyes, a lot like a smartphone. He set it down on the table and it projected an image into the air above it. Jed found himself looking at a very unpleasant creature. It was humanoid, barely, with four arms, and covered in a nasty-looking orange, rough skin. The head was flattened, with a mouth that stretched from ear hole to ear hole. The effect was rather like a newt he had once seen.

"This is a G'his. They were a roving band of bandits, raiding and running, until about forty years ago, when they decided to start empire building. They have been attempting to conquer and destroy our people. We have three planets that we inhabit. They have done much damage on one, and we fear that we will not be able to hold them off. The Orion'ess are not a warlike race. We lack the aggressiveness necessary. But humans, whom we have come to admire as a race, have the knowledge of war we think could defeat the G'his. We have come to ask for help."

Jed nodded. This he could understand Mind you, he didn't think it was the whole truth, but that wasn't his problem. "It isn't my place to say whether we will or not, but I have an idea that you will get some help. Even if the government says no, there will always be men like me who will not turn down the offer of travel to exotic locales to help the underdog out."

He continued, "I think what you want from me is a contact point to reach the government?"

"Yes. We knew that by contacting you, we would reach the military, and your military, of course, is most likely to give us the advice we need to begin properly fighting the G'his. But we also want to set up friendly contact with Earth. A chance to gain an ally and friend is never something to scoff at."

Jed grimaced at the thoughts that "military advice" brought to mind. But he realized there had to be more to it. The Orion'ess no doubt knew that the US of A was loyal to its allies, which was why they had been contacted first, and as a race, he suspected the Orion'ess were pretty shrewd. They had to know that a federation of races would better be able to fend off space bandits. But what was the reason behind the symbiote? And just who had the men who had chased then to Oscar's cabin been? Where were the Cats in all this? His mind swirled with questions, but it was the first he asked.

A'lina replied after a brief conference between the other two. "We think the 'Cats' as you call them intended it as a sign of their capabilities, and as a gift. A proof of their - and indeed, our, sincerity, as you will. They are a part of our Alliance."

"Then you might want to rethink giving us any more gifts." Jed said grimly. "One man is dead because of it. The - er - container the spores were in exploded and injured two and killed one. The injuries healed quickly enough, as the symbiote did its work, but it is still a problem."

"Oh, no!" A'lina's skin dulled, and he guessed this was akin to a human skin pallor. "We had no idea. I am so very sorry."

"We intend to share our technology with your race." said A'fri. "But it was never our intention to cause any harm. I hope you can accept that."

"I understand." Jed reassured them. "But you may want to apologize to the man's family."

"Of course."

"Now, did you have more questions for us, or would you like to return and make a report to your superiors?"

"Yes, I would like to do that." Jed said gratefully. He was feeling a bit overwhelmed. They seemed nice enough, if somewhat clumsy, but he knew he was out of his depth here.

They walked him out of the craft. He asked what it was, and what it was called, and they told him it was an unarmed scout ship, and that in a far Earth orbit, there was a much larger survey ship that they had come in from.

"It's type is called a ... a Hyless." A'lita said. She added rather doubtfully, "That is our word. I do not know what it would translate to."

As they stopped, Jed turned and with some hesitation, asked "Would it be rude to ask you what you really look like? Under your cloaks?"

A'fri smiled. "No, we wore the cloaks to reduce the impact of our difference on you. These are usually only cold-weather wear."

He threw back the cloak and spread his arms. Jed sucked in his breath. They had wings. It was not a structure with which they could actually fly, but they were gliders, he had no doubt. A framework of bone, over which was stretched a thin, iridescent membrane, covered in places with something that was either feather or scale, he couldn't decide which. A'fri grinned and elevated a crest on his head, showing off his feather/scales there, which Jed had not noticed before. He wore clothes, a long fall of fabric down his chest and back, caught at the groin and fitted almost like trousers around the legs. His wing membrane was attached from shoulder to hip, and this area was left open on his tunic. A'lina spread her wings then, showing him that she was much smaller than A'fri, something he had noted before, and she wore a more dress-like costume. She showed him that she and A'lita had a short, close-lying layer of the feather/scales over their scalps. All three of them had very long, slender bodies, with no fat layers that he could tell. Jed thanked them and set off for his camp, feeling bemused. This time yesterday he would have said that his mission would find nothing, and the rapidity if which things were happening was making his head spin.

When he got back to his little tent, he pulled out the satellite phone, deciding to access his voice mail first. When he heard Gabi's voice, a rush of emotion tumbled over him. Joy at hearing her, concern at the fatigue in her voice, and confusion at how she had been able to leave a message box only Colonel Matthewson normally had access to. As he listened to her relate the events that had followed the human trials, though, he was horrified.

What can I do? he asked himself. As well-meaning as the Orion'ess may have been, this shoots it right down the crapper. They are going to be viewed as dangerous. And Gabi will not be pleased... What am I going to do about this? He came to a decision quickly.

He scooped up the phone and ran back to the Hyless. He was not going to make a report until he found out how the Orion'ess would react to this information. A'fri must have seen him coming, because he met him at the ramp. He gestured for Jed to follow him back into the room they had been in before. John set the phone down on the table and replayed the message for him. A'fri listened intently, slowly losing his iridescence. When it was finished he turned to the females, who had joined them a moment after Jed's arrival. he spoke quickly and at some length to them in their tongue, answering the occasional question from one or the other of them. At length, he turned back to Jed.

"This is a grave complication. We never expected that you would try to pass the symbiote on in this manner. It was not designed for this, but for the long term - to be passed on through your normal reproductive patterns. But by attempting to force the organism into the bloodstream, you have antagonized the immune system. I am amazed that you were successful at all. But the damage that has been caused in the survivors may be mitigated by some of our medical techniques. Would that be acceptable?"

"I think so. I have not yet made my report, what do you want me to tell Dr. McGregor?"

A'lina spoke now. "I think it would be better to do it myself. I am a medical person, and I am qualified to do this. Dr. McGregor may mean well, but I can do this much easier than I can explain for her to do."

She spoke to A'fri, then when he nodded and left the room, she turned back to Jed. "We are going to go to this place where your injured are. Can you guide us?"

"Well, for starters, it is on a military base, and if you just fly in they will shoot at you, and secondly, no, I do not know the exact coordinates."

"Can you ask for permission?"

"I can try." Jed said rather dubiously.

He picked up the handset and took a deep breath. This was going to be interesting.

Two and a half hours later they were in the air. It had taken Jed almost two hours to talk the colonel through what had happened, and then to persuade him to allow the alien craft onto the base. Only Jed's personal pledge that the craft was unarmed finally won through. The colonel had growled something to the effect of have you got a gun to your head? but Jed had convinced him that this was real and imperative. Then Jed took a little time to break his camp, before returning to the Hyless and stowing it into a locker they gave him. A'fri invited him to meet the others of the crew and ride in the cockpit. Jed followed him into a small area with barely enough room for four Orion'ess. Jed's broad shoulders made the space a bit cramped, but the two Orion'ess there greeted him cheerfully enough. They both bowed to him from their seats and introduced themselves as N'edh and J'ron. A'fri showed Jed how to use the restraints and explained as the engines warmed up that the Hyless usually carried a five person crew. He gave the coordinates to the pilot, N'edh, and they lifted slowly off the ground, straight up. When they had reached a significant altitude, they suddenly accelerated forward and up. Jed was pushed back into his seat, and shortly realized with amazement that they were at the outer edge of the atmosphere. The acceleration slowed, there was an instant of stomach-churning null gravity, and then they began to glide downward again.

"Wow," he managed after a minute to be sure his lunch would stay down. "That is a wild ride."

A'fri smiled at him, and Jed realized he had not heard any of them laugh. They would smile, but evidently did not laugh. "It works something like your scoop-jet recently pioneered. We use a different propulsion in space, of course."

"Don't bother explaining it to me. I'm not up on the Aerospace developments. If you want escape and evasion, I'm your guy." Something occurred to him then. "Hey, how come you can talk directly to me?"

A'fri grinned and showed Jed the electronic device that he carried in his upper pocket. "The computer generates my voice in English for you. We used A'lita as a translator before as a mark of formality and because it is much more intimate than communicating through a computer."

A'fri and Jed continued to talk about the technology, in particular the method of silent communication Jed had seen A'lita use. Jed was so interested he was surprised to hear N'edh ask how he should approach the base. "With as much fanfare as possible." Jed suggested drily.

When Jed walked down the ramp, shading his eyes against the bright sunlight, the first thing he saw was Gabi, running across the tarmac toward him. The Colonel was following her at a more dignified pace, accompanied by Paul Monroe.

Gabi threw herself into Jed's arms, almost knocking him over. He hugged her convulsively, renewing his vow to never leave her again as she turned a tear-wet face up to him and kissed him soundly. When they separated, he realized there was quite a crowd gathered to see their first alien spaceship. There were cheers and whistles as he waved at them and thoroughly kissed Gabi again. She was blushing when he let her go again.

"I'm not leaving you again." he told her. "And if you run away I'm going after you."

As Colonel Matthewson came up, Jed saluted him sharply, and then told him, "Sir, with all due respect, I am retiring."

Matthewson laughed and shook his hand. "I thought so. I still have you for 22 days, though," he warned.

Jed remembered why they were there, and turned back to where three cloaked figure were waiting at the top of the ramp. "Sir, these are the Orion'ess. They have come to Earth hoping to set up an embassy and to ask our help on some matters." he repeated some of the things he had already told the colonel, and then A'fri stepped forward and gravely bowed to him. Colonel Robin Matthewson bowed back. "Welcome to Earth." he said.

Evaluations

Early the next morning Gabi met A'lina at the lab. A'lina wore a pristine white tunic, and looked like a professional to Gabi's eyes. Gabi bowed to her, and smiled.

"I hear you may be able to help me with my patients."

A'lina smiled back. "I am so very pleased to meet you, Dr. McGregor. Yes, I think I can improve their prognosis. Would you let me see them?"

"Follow me." Gabi walked into the big room where the survivors lay, feeling encouraged for the first time since that horrible day. "Two of them have the symbiote in their bloodstream now. One came through with no apparent complications, the other sustained brain damage when his fever peaked at about 109. He is healing rapidly, but the damage is evident in - strange ways."

The patients, those who still thought coherently, turned to look at them. Charles Drentz, dressed in his lab coat and standing by a bed, looked guilty.

"Gabrielle, really, I feel fine." He protested as she took his elbow and led him back to his bed.

He sat on the edge of the bed and then saw Gabi's companion. His eyes lit up. "Welcome. You must be one of the Orion'ess."

"Yes, I am A'lina. And you must be Charles Drentz. Dr. McGregor told me of you yesterday." she bowed gracefully to him and continued. "I am so sorry for the losses you suffered in this trial. We ought to have contacted humans at once, but we were curious to find out how you would react to us, so we sent the symbiote ahead to herald our arrival. We never expected you to try to spread the symbiote like this."

A look of pain crossed his face. "I am sorry I allowed myself to be talked into the trial so rapidly. My greatest flaw is that I forget myself in research, and I forgot the humanity of my subjects in this case. My vanity allowed me to become a test subject myself, and not to realize that Dr. Lewiston meant to take the symbiote on himself." He sighed and looked at Gabi. "I am sorry."

She took his shoulder. "'Tis past, Charles. A'lina may be able to help."

"There are six men with brain damage. They all show different levels of encephalography, from non reactive, to automatic but inappropriate reactions. The one in best condition is Dr. Lewiston. I upgraded him this morning. It is apparent that his symbiote is assisting his recovery. The others are progressing slowly, if at all. I think we were lucky to save any of them. Adult humans do not often have to endure this high a fever unless it is due to heat stroke."

A'lina opened her kit and took out two flexible white pads. "May I?" she said, indicating Gabi's temples.

Startled, Gabi hesitated, then assented. "Why?" she asked as A'lina fixed them to her head.

"I need a normal scan to compare with the patients. I do not think your brains are the same as Orion'ess."

"True." Gabi agreed. "Although I don't know how normal mine is, with the symbiote. Carlos." she called.

"Yes, Doctor?" he appeared at her elbow.

"Would you mind letting A'lina scan your brain so she can compare a healthy brain to the patients?"

He looked warily at A'lina, but her peaceful beauty seemed to reassure him. "All right, ma'am." he finally gave in.

After a moment, A'lina took the pads from Gabi and put them on Carlos's head. Gabi asked, "Where do you read the information?"

The unworldly beauty pulled a small computer out of her kit and opened up the screen to show Gabi. Folded, it was about half the size of a sheet of paper, and unfolded, it was all screen, with a small speaker in one corner. A'lina spoke to it, a command that was not translated by the electronic module she wore, and the information it was downloading about Carlos's brain flashed onto the screen. A'lina touched one line, and it froze. Gabi realized there was no need for a keyboard because it was entirely voice and touch operated.

"Very nice."

"I am ready to test the patients now."

Together Gabi and A'lina worked their way from bed to bed, Gabi soothing with voice or touch, even the unresponsive patient. A'lina commented on this, watching the reaction of their brains to the human doctor's touch.

"See, here," she said, showing Gabi the spiky graph of one man, who tossed in his bed muttering incoherently until Gabi smoothed his forehead and called him by name. "The waves show a definite calming when you touch him. Remarkable. We - the Orion'ess - do not often touch - not like you humans. You are healing just by this personal contact. Did you do this deliberately?"

Gabi flushed. "No, it just seemed right. You see, I am a research doc. I don't often have much to do with actual human subjects. I felt responsible for these men, felt that I ought to have fought harder for the trial to be postponed. I started touching them to apologize, really, for the pain they were going through."

"When you touch them, the brain emits a substance - the same thing I thought to give them, in larger quantities, to hasten their recovery."

They came at last to David Lewiston, and Gabi saw at a glance that he was much better, sitting up in his bed and glaring at them. "No!" he said when A'lina attempted to place the pads on him "I don't know how you were given clearance to get in here, but I will not submit to be - tampered with!"

"David," Gabi said placating him, "She needs to see what condition your brain is in before we can treat you."

"I will not be treated by this, this - alien." he spat out, his face paling as he pressed back into his pillow.

"Really, Dr. Lewiston," Gabi said tartly. "Xenophobia in a man of your intelligence."

He looked daggers at her, then turned to A'lina. "All right. Do what you need to," he closed his eyes, pale, and did not open them again until she had walked away from his bedside.

When they had monitored all of the men, Gabi took A'lina back into the lab.

A'lina pulled up the results, showing Gabi what she was doing and how to do it.

They compared the results and decided on a course of medication to best heal each individual. It took them two more days of tinkering in the lab to develop the drugs needed. On the third day A'lina and Gabi turned their attention to the symbiont enhanced results. A'lina lingered longest over Gabi's results, and then compared them to Charles's. Then she pulled up the results Dr. Lewiston had given her so reluctantly.

"Look, here." she pointed. "The symbiote has elevated your memory. Had you noticed?"

"Not really... yes, I have." Gabi looked up in surprise. "I have always remembered easily - studying in school was simple for me compared to most of my friends. But since the symbiote, I need only look at something once to get a clear picture that I remember completely."

"The symbiote is enhancing you. I think." she wrinkled her nose as she peered more closely at the scans of Gabi's brain. "It looks as though you have elevated activity here, and here..." she indicated the memory centers, and another area. "Have you noticed increased reaction time?"

"No, but Jed and Paul have been doing a lot of physical testing. Perhaps we should ask them."

As they walked down the hall, A'lina asked, "Why did both of your senior doctors volunteer for such a potentially harmful experiment?"

Gabi sighed. "When Dr. Lewiston was trying to reassure me of the safety of the trial, he offered to add either himself or Dr. Drentz to the list of participants. I was dubious, but it wasn't my decision. It wasn't until the interns were doing the injections that I realized that Dr. Lewiston meant to be injected himself no matter what, and the first problems began to happen so quickly I could not remonstrate with him."

They met Colonel Matthewson in the hall and he walked with them, chatting to them about the recovery of the men, some of whom had been under his command. A'lina assured them that the drug she had ordered for them should encourage regeneration of lost cells. "But," she cautioned, "They will not regain any memory that was stored in the tissue that was damaged. Some of them may still require extensive rehabilitation."

The colonel snorted. "Ma'am, if they can have normal lives again, it doesn't matter. I am just happy none of them will be vegetables, which Dr. McGregor said might be the case if you had not offered your help."

He knew where the men were, and led them to a pool that Gabi had not even

known was there. Paul and Jed were in it,
not swimming, but seeming to be sitting
at the bottom of the pool.

"What on earth?" asked Gabi, leaning
over the side to better see them.

A few men were hanging around, and
one of them had a stopwatch. He trotted
over, grinning. "Been down there ten
minutes and thirty-five seconds."

Gabi whipped around to glare at him.
"And you haven't gone in after them?"

"Oh, no, ma'am." he assured her, eyes
wide. "Captain McGregor'd have my hide.
He said they'd be fine, just to keep good
time. Yesterday they were down there
almost a half-hour. He said he wanted to
see how long they could go."

She spluttered, "Haven't you ever
heard of hypoxia? They could pass out and
you wouldn't even know it!"

A'lina asked "Has the symbiote
enhanced the oxygen carrying abilities of
your red blood cells?"

"Yes, we noticed that, but this
is...." she waved her hand at the pool in
frustration.

"It was designed to enable you to go
without breathing for an extended time."

Gabi tried to calm down. "I see."

She sat down on the edge of a bench
and started to take off her shoes,
sensible walking shoes someone had given
her, since she had arrived with no
wearable clothing. Then she pulled off

her lab coat and uniform blouse. Walking
to the edge of the pool, clad in fatigue
pants, brown t-shirt and socks, she
stepped over the edge and dropped in.
With a little effort, she got the air out
of her pants and swam to where they were.
Jed saw her and grinned. Paul waved
hello. She saw that both of them had a
weight belt on, and were sitting
comfortably cross-legged. They each
grabbed an arm and helped her stay down.
She blinked, surprised not to feel a need
to take a breath. She had been a good
swimmer once, but the years in Alaska had
left her with little chance to skin dive
or even swim.

Gabrielle made a mental note to study
sign language with them if they intended
to do this often. It was frustrating not
to be able to talk, and besides, if they
ever really needed to do this, a method
of communication would be a good thing.
She drifted calmly, wondering at the ease
with which she was thinking, feeling no
pain in her lungs for lack of air.
Finally, Jed jerked his thumb toward the
surface, and he and Paul released their
weight belts and the three of them kicked
off for air. Gabi found that she breathed
easily on the surface, not needing to
gulp and gasp for air as she would have
before. The soldier with the stopwatch
gave them a helping hand out of the pool.

"Thirty-four minutes and seven seconds," he announced, beaming.

"You should not have tried this experiment without supervision!" Gabi rounded on Paul and Jed. "What if you had passed out down there?"

"Hey!" protested Paul, "We aren't stupid..."

Jed just chuckled and kissed her, cutting off her response to Paul's comment. When he let her go, he said "Isn't it amazing to be able to do what we just did?"

"Well, yes."

"Don't forget to wonder at life, instead of just studying the why's and wherefore's." he said softly, kissing her forehead. "Now you might want to go change out of these wet clothes."

Take me to Your Leader

She walked away, and Jed turned to Colonel Matthewson. "What do you think, sir?"

"Very impressive," he nodded at A'lina, who was standing quietly to one side, watching them all. "The Orion'ess have offered to give us a lift to their appointment to meet the President. I am looking forward to riding in that slick plane." his eyes twinkled.

"Us, sir?"

"Yes, the President wants to meet you 'supermen', too. I am going along to brief the Joint Chiefs, but I wouldn't have missed this for the world anyway. Dr. Lewiston will be coming along," he turned to Gabi, who was rejoining them then. "The President wants to see for himself that his first choice for Surgeon General is back up to speed. He wants to push the appointment through soon."

"But Dr. Lewiston isn't ready yet. We don't know how much permanent memory loss he may have, or what other effects there may be." Gabi protested.

Colonel Matthewson just shrugged. "'Tis not mine to reason why." he quoted. "Dr. Drentz will be coming along to monitor him."

"Very well. When are we expected?"

"Tomorrow morning about nine. Evidently that gives us all time to meet, and time for him to arrange to keep this secret. He doesn't like that, though."

Gabi made a face, and Jed chuckled. "He is, after all, a politician," Jed reminded them. Jed thought reminiscently of his irritation at the time the current ultra-liberal president had been elected, and how as a soldier he was bound to be loyal to the man. "I will be glad to retire," he said aloud, fervently. This sent everyone off into gales of laughter, as they guessed his thoughts from the look on his face.

That thought boiled through his mind late the next day as he stood behind a podium next to Gabi and smiling stiffly. He would be so glad to get away from the military, to be able to call himself a free man once more. They had landed that morning, rather spectacularly, next to the Washington Monument, camouflaged well enough that no-one could have guessed that they were there. It was a beautiful, crisp fall day with bright sun and brilliant blue sky. The White House people had been giddy over the prospect of beautiful photographs of the 'alien spacecraft' next to the newly restored monument. They had not, to his mind, been at all awed by the reality of extraterrestrial beings landing on

American soil. Jed thought of the flighty
aides who had met them and led them off
to their separate briefings. He wasn't
sure that they accepted the reality of
the situation at all. But he wasn't sure
that he blamed them, brought up on the X-
files and suchlike as they were. The day
had been spent in meetings, as Gabi
presented the findings about the symbiote
and it's enhancements on their bodies.
Paul and he had not had much to say. Now
they were meeting with the President
himself, and the Orioness.

They stood, he and Paul and Gabi,
behind the departing Surgeon General, and
David Lewiston, who was a shoo-in as his
replacement. The medical minutiae had
been discussed, and the Surgeon General
was taking follow-up questions. The
President shook his gaunt, greying head
and asked, "So if I follow you, this bug
alters the gene structure to make their
bodies do what it wants them to do?"

"Yes, we have seen genetic alteration
in several areas, chiefly in the genes
that regulate aging. The aging process
has been slowed, and perhaps even
reversed."

Jed looked at Gabi. They knew full
well it had been reversed. Jed's body had
been slowing , responding to the strains
of years of hard training and injuries,
but since the symbiote, his body was
stronger, scar tissue disappearing,

replaced by young, flexible cells that responded as a much younger man's would.

The Surgeon General continued. "there would also seem to be some genetic alteration when the gene for a certain disease is found. One of the persons infected had diabetes, but has been cured by this genetic alteration. The problem is..." he paused for full effect of his next words. "It is immune specific to these three, the original vectors of the... symbiote. That means that it cannot be easily transferred to others, without fear of an allergic reaction."

Gabi winced, and Jed knew what she was thinking. Society was skeptical at best of genetically altered animals and plants, how was it going to respond to genetically altered humans? Further, what would society say to the fact that the symbiote could not be easily shared with the general public, but was engineered to be passed down to the children of those originally infected? He was relieved when Dr. Lewiston's interview ended, and the three of them faced the man himself. He looked the three of them up and down, but did not offer his hand. Gabi felt a shudder of premonition run up and down her spine. Finally he asked if they would mind waiting in the next room until he had spoken with the Orioness.

Stony faced, Jed saluted and marched out. Gabi, walking behind him, could read his disgust in every movement. She couldn't remember the last time she had seen him move with such deliberate precision. Two Secret Servicemen followed them into the anteroom and took up positions flanking the door as it closed. Gabi felt the fear rising up in her chest, choking her. Eyes wide, she turned and looked up at Jed, but he only shook his head, a grim expression on his face. Paul, too, looked pale, and he stood beside Gabi looking up at the older man. Jed cursed under his breath, fluidly, in a language Gabi did not recognize.

"I am responsible to you two, but my honor is pledged to... that." he jerked his head toward the other room. Gabi had to strain to hear him, and yet she understood completely. As a warrior, he had pledged himself in service to his country, and the figurehead of their country was a man who did not believe in war, and who had been afraid of them - of the things they carried in their bloodstreams. Gabi had seen it in his eyes, and she knew the others had, too. Now they could only wait and wonder what their fate would be.

A door opened behind her and Gabi jumped. She turned and saw Dr. Drentz. Her smile of welcome died on her face at his expression.

"I have been asked to wait in here with you." he said simply, but Gabi could see the concern in his eyes. She gave him a quick hug, and he retuned it with a grateful look. "Also, I was asked to back up Dr. Lewiston's statement that he does not carry the symbiote. Since he does not, I said yes, and then they wanted to know if anyone else in the party had it, and when I told them that I was the only one, they told - asked - me to wait with you."

"It isn't good, is it?" whispered Gabi.

No-one answered. No one had to. They all knew that the man who was now in charge of the most powerful nation on the planet had decided they were a danger. Now they were waiting to find out what he was going to do with them.

Return of the Mongols

"Earth... it will be a diadem in my crown, will it not, Mariss?"

The ship drifted far above the Planet, and all he could see were the swirling colors of clouds, continents, and oceans. He breathed deeply, savoring the thought of clear, fresh air as though he could really smell it, and not the foul air of the ship. The original creators of the ship were long gone, generations before, and with them had gone some of the knowledge of maintaining the ship. Oh, the systems necessary to its function were kept up, of course. But in the back of everyone's mind was the knowledge that anytime they earned it, they could move up to a better, newer ship.

The female snorted. "But you do not like planets. Hah! I'd never catch you staying longer than you have to on one!"

He smiled. The reason this female accompanied him so often was her spirit, which had not waned since he had taken her two cycles before. He felt that a good argument cleared the mind, and so she was his favorite. He stroked her head, absently, as it was knee-level and a very easy place to reach. Her soft

purple crest flattened with satisfaction
and she lifted her triangular face up to
look at his expression. Seeing that it
held no anger, she continued "Why is this
one so special?"

"We are the first race to contact it,
and they have no - well, very limited -
space travel. And they are an industrial
world."

"Oh... how nice."

And now the two of them had matching
expressions, looking down at the waiting
planet below.

A chime sounded, and he murmured
"Yes?"

"Fleet Prince Frisst, the fleet is in
position."

"Very well Captain, I will join you
in the Combat deck directly."

Mariss looked up from her keeling
position at his feet. She could not move
or stand until he released her, and she
was hoping that he would allow her to
return to quarters until he was ready for
her company again. He smiled lazily down
at her, his smile crinkling up his large,
almond-shaped black eyes. His round face
with its epicanthic folds and fringe of
black hair would have brought a jolt of
instant recognition to any inhabitant of
the planet below, for he was the very
image of an ancient Mongol. But Mariss, a
species from a planet further away than
any human had dreamed of before, did not

know and would not have cared just then.
He owned her body and soul, and she had
no choice but to wait until he released
her collar. Finally, he did so, smiling
still at the terror in her eyes. She
hated to be chained like this, but he
kept her restrained now anywhere outside
of their quarters. She had tried to
escape once too often, and she knew she
was lucky he hadn't punished her more...
permanently.

After escorting his slave to their
shared quarters, Frisst made his way to
the combat deck, stepping happily in to
view his plans unfold. The sphere of
holograph that showed all his fleet cast
its greenish glow over the whole room. At
stations all around the walls, men and
women worked at hooded consoles, to keep
any light from blurring the projection.
The green dots that were his ships were
clustered at one side of the planet in
the holo, but he could see at once that
they had already begun to creep away from
one another, out into the pattern that
would enfold the Earth before too long.
But Frisst would not be on this ship when
they did so. He had a dinner invitation
to the the White House of the USA.

"Very good, Captain Rii." he said
now, circling the holosphere. "Everything
appears to be going smoothly?"

"Yes, Fleet Prince. All the ships
will reach their targets on schedule.

Your shuttle is ready in Bay 1, as well, sir."

"Ah. Well, I suppose I must prepare to meet these humans in time for their 'newscasts'. How... fortunate that they have such a global communication network. It will serve beautifully to get the word out of our arrival and friendly intentions."

"Yes, Fleet Prince." the other acknowledged woodenly. Frisst knew the man hated having him in the Combat deck, so he continued to stand and stare into the holosphere for a long moment before dismissing the man and leaving the deck. Behind him, there was a collective sigh of relief. Ever since Frisst had inherited the ship from his older brother, they had lived in fear of his capricious rages.

Frisst hummed happily as he made his way to the shuttle bay. Waiting for him there were his cousins, the newly created Ambassador to Earth and Frisst's military advisor. Also standing rigidly beside the shuttle were his body guards. the captain of the guard snapped him a salute, and Frisst returned it casually.

"Captain Bletti, must I remind you again of the protocol for this Earth visit?" he asked with some exasperation in his voice.

"No, Fleet Prince." the captain bared his teeth in a smile. "I merely wanted my guard and I to show our honor at being chosen to accompany you on this occasion of... opportunity."

Frisst threw back his head and laughed. His guard, as some of the first to make contact, would gain a greater share of the prize moneys later. He had chosen well with Captain Bletti, indeed. No compassion here, to possibly endanger Frisst's plans.

"Very well then. Let us proceed."

Frisst smiled for longer that evening than he had ever done before. He found himself reflecting on that as he sipped the admirable wine that was served with the sumptuous meal the United States President had fed them. He was ostensibly listening to the man talking about Earth, and how the United States had been the right choice for the G'his to contact first, but his mind was wandering. Who could have known, when he was assigned this sector, that such a ripe plum of a planet awaited him? The Orioness may have thought they had their data on this planet well hidden, but G'his techs could find anything in a database.

He smiled again at the President and murmured "Yes, Mister President, I think the United States will be the perfect liaison between us and your beautiful world."

Indeed, Frisst thought, this nation's power could be used in very interesting ways. The Fleet might not have to expend much effort at all to reap this world's bounty. The vaunted liberties of this place would become hollow with what he had to bribe their leaders with. Now, where to begin. He smiled more broadly and leaned over the table slightly.

"I understand there are some... security issues your nation has been dealing with. This is a problem, as we have a preference for trading with somewhat more... stable worlds. However, some of the technologies we can offer you may help."

"Really?" The man's eyes sparkled, although Frisst thought he was also surprised at the abruptness of his offer. Well, no sense in prolonging the thing. Cut to the chase, and be first at the kill. He beamed at the human.

"Yes. I understand that you have not been successful in defeating them before this by direct methods..."

And that, Frisst thought, was because this man was a fool. His predecessor had kept things under control, but this man, with his concerns over offending fellow nations and spending too much, had hamstrung the United States in their efforts to rid themselves of the religious fanatics that threatened them. Frisst himself would have advocated an even more direct approach than the earlier President, but humans were soft.

He settled into preliminary negotiations with the man who was walking right into his arms.

****

Two months later, many of the six billion biochips the G'his had brought with them were inside the humans of Earth. New laws in almost every nation required them, for they were what Earth's new friends used to track everyone, and yet they had sworn not to reveal the information to anyone on Earth. Anyone who resisted the biochips was courteously allowed to leave the registration centers... and then discovered that all their assets were frozen, policemen eyed them suspiciously, and they could no longer vote.

Huge protests against what most saw as the ultimate violation of their privacy - and by strangers, to boot - were virtually ignored. Those who protested were no longer constituents, and had no voice. Also, their numbers grew smaller and smaller as they faced hunger and persecution.

Violence peaked, and then fell. By the time the G'his had been in orbit for a year, Earth was One Nation, under control, and a "suitably stable environment for Galactic Trade" as one G'his Ambassador put it.

Flight in Fear

"We have to take you off the planet. The G'his are here already."

Gabi shook her head, not comprehending what A'lita had just told her. "What... what do you mean, the G'his?"

"The other alien race that had contacted your government. They are arriving in Earth orbit and they are not friendly, Gabi. If they find you, and the others with the symbiote, they will know we have been here, and we cannot allow that to happen now. We had intended to give all your military personnel the symbiote, but that chance has gone, and now we have to retreat. Please... my entire race depends on them not detecting us now."

A'lita reached out and took Gabi's hands in hers, clasping them lightly to her chest. Gabi could feel the increased respiration and pulse, and realized that A'lita was serious. "But... but I can't just leave Earth! This is my home! And Jed, and Paul... what will we all do?"

Gabi knew she was being irrational, but the shock of the past few days was crashing in on her. First the rebuff of the President, the quarantine of all those with the symbiote, and now being

asked to leave her home for parts
unknown. She reeled, her head spinning.
With a high trill, A'lita caught her, and
Gabi could hear her calling for Jed over
her head as she lost consciousness.

When she opened her eyes again she
was in a reclined chair in the Hyless,
with A'lina leaning over her.

"Ah!" she said cheerfully. "You have
had entirely too much stress on your
system, Madame Doctor. Now lie still and
rest."

"Where are we?" Gabi asked, trying to
sit up. A'lina prevented her. "Please, my
friend, try to just rest, and do not
think for a while."

"Well," Gabi began, but she was so
tired, so very tired of going on and on
and not finding the answers. "All right,"
she finished faintly.

"Good." A'lina straightened and said
briskly. "I will take care of the
arrangements. Lie still and rest, please.
I will send Paul or Jed to you as soon as
they have helped me finish the plans for
your evacuation."

****
***

"How did she take it?" Jed asked as
A'lina slipped into the small, now
crowded, conference room.

"Well. She is very tired and is resting now. Now, what have you come up with?"

"We are going to run, in stealth, to the [ch'liss]..."

"The what?" Jed interrupted.

"Um, I think it translates closest to 'carrier'. The term 'mother-ship' as used by your popular folklore is also close, but the connotation..."

"Yeah, carrier is good." Jed answered with a chuckle. "Go on."

"And then run like hell to get out of system before the G'his think to look too closely for any other ships. Right now they are under the illusion that no-one else has interstellar capability but them, but I am afraid that is an illusion that may collapse at any time."

A'lina spread her arms slightly, her wings making flashes of light fill the cabin. A'fri stopped and looked at her.

"No, we must make a detour first. We must go to Alaska and pick up Gabi's family. I have already arranged for Paul's family to be evacuated. Jed, am I correct in thinking you have no close relatives?"

"Yes, I have a couple of distant cousins, that's all. What are you thinking?"

"I do not know when we will be able to return you to Earth. There is a distinct possibility that we will never

be able to. I do not want the three of
you to be lonely, and I want to give
humans a chance - a separate breeding
pool, if you will."

Paul blinked and shuddered. "Is it
going to be that bad?"

"Yes. The G'his have been known to
reduce entire populations to ash rather
than bother to subdue them. The Orioness
have been beaten too badly to come to the
rescue of Earth now. In five or ten
years, perhaps, but not yet. We must
withdraw, and recoup to try again. And
that means that you, the evidence of our
presence here, must not be found."

"I gathered that." Jed interjected
drily.

A'lina shrugged. "So, I feel
responsible for your exile, and I want to
be sure that you have a chance. And, to
be frank, I am looking forward to working
with Gabi." She twinkled a little, and
made the musical chiming sound that they
were learning to recognize as the
Orioness laughter.

"Well, it sounds like you have
everything well in hand, milady." Jed
said ironically, offering her a little
bow. "Now, as I was telling A'fri, I want
to organize a resistance here on Earth."

Paul asked "You mean stay behind?"

"No, but I want to give Colonel
Matthewson a complete briefing on the

situation. If anyone can do something when the shit hits the fan, he can."

A'fri nodded. "Yes, that will be a good thing, since we need to ask him to suppress what is known about you three, and to kidnap the others with the symbiote. So, we will take you and Gabi on the Hyless, Paul, you will go to Alaska on the F'lessa with A'lita to get Gabi's family, and we will meet you there, along with the J'ssa, which is in New England getting Paul's family."

"How are you persuading them to come along without Paul being there?" Jed asked curiously.

"We have already had contacts with them. They are ready to come."

"Oh."

J'red put his head into the cabin. "The F'lessa is here, Ambassador A'fri. Are we ready?"

"Yes. Paul?"

He nodded and they all stood, allowing him and A'lita to go out. A'lina put a hand on Jed's sleeve. "Wait a moment."

"Yes?" he bent his head to hear her low tone better.

"I need to talk to you and Gabi as soon as I can. Once we are airborne, perhaps?"

"Certainly."

She left, and Jed stood looking down the corridor, feeling puzzled. Then he went back into the conference cabin and sat down, his brain whirling. Somehow he had to get all this to Colonel Matthewson and figure out the best way to make life difficult for the G'his without antagonizing them into using their weapons. What were their weapons, anyway? He sighed and pulled out his personal data unit to begin jotting down his notes. Mostly questions, but then at least he would know what he didn't know.

He was still working on this when he felt the motion of the ship - a lot like the feel of a jetliner, he mused. I wonder if this is it? He was expecting to feel weightless any minute now... but then the "push" stopped and he still felt normal. He stood up and went toward the corridor, wondering if there had been a problem. He poked his head out into the corridor, and saw A'lina coming out of the tiny sick bay where Gabi had been since she fainted.

"Ah! There you are. I was just coming to get you."

"Have we lifted off? Is there a problem?"

"Yes, we are on our way. You will not feel the lack of gravity because all our ships have the means to use their inertia to compensate for the lack of gravity - or, for that matter, the presence of it, when we lift off for instance."

Jed grinned. Even if he hadn't known that A'lina was the equivalent of a university professor, he could have guessed from her speech. Amazing how understandable aliens were. At least, he amended himself, these aliens are.

Then he went in to Gabi and knelt beside her. She looked a little pale, but she smiled at him when he came in the door and that was what mattered. "Hey," he brushed her hair gently away from her face, "how are you feeling?"

"Ok. Just... stunned. I can't believe we are leaving Earth. It's like having a bad dream I can't wake up from."

"How about a grand adventure? The unknown waits for us. We have friends with us, and one another."

She chuckled. "You are right. I don't know what is wrong with me... I just feel so nervous and hesitant."

A'lina interrupted. "If I may?"

They looked up at her, and she beamed down at them. "I believe what Gabi is feeling is an instinctual reaction generated by the pregnancy hormones currently in her body. I can give you the specifics if you would like, Gabrielle..."

Jed felt like someone had hit him on the head with a two-by-four. "Wh-what?"

He looked down at Gabi for confirmation and she looked back at him with wide eyes. She hadn't known either.

He saw the understanding in her eyes then. "We should have known... we knew that you were, um, intact again. It was only a matter of time."

"When?" he finally managed, breathing deeply. He couldn't remember ever feeling quite this afraid. He had done some fearsome things in his life, and many of them had scared him silly, but nothing like "I'm going to be a daddy." he said aloud.

He laughed, and hugged her. She clung to him in return and whispered. "Oh, Jed, this baby is going to need us so much... We haven't even got a home for it."

She looked up at A'lina after a moment. Her friend had stepped away and turned her head to give them a little privacy. "A'lina?"

"Yes, Gabi?"

The Orioness lady was beaming. Gabi recalled something she had picked up in passing . Children were a rare event with the Orioness. Their population grew slowly - part of the reason the G'his had been so devastating to them, even though their planet had not been destroyed. She smiled back at her new friend. "Can we tell how far along I am?"

She looked thoughtful "I am not sure. We have not had the opportunity to study a pregnant woman. But from the medical texts I think I can figure it out. Or you can."

Gabi grimaced. "I haven't studied many pregnant women either. Not my field of medicine, more's the pity."

Jed looked from one to the other. "But how about when she gives birth? Will there be someone who knows then?"

"Oh, yes, "A'lina reassured him. "The human and Orioness physiology is very similar in this area, and besides that, when we are all together on the, ah, carrier, Paul's mother is an accomplished midwife. Her name is Margaret. Now, as far as determining your gestation..."

She picked up a small instrument and made some adjustments to it, and then spoke Orioness into it for a moment. Jed was reminded forcibly of a 'tricorder' or what ever that thing was called on Star Trek. As A'lina began to run it over Gabi's abdomen, she explained that not only did this 'thing' perform various soft tissue scans, like the close relative to a sonogram that she was doing now, but it was a recorder for the doctor's notes, which were then transmitted to a central location. Gabi nodded. "So keeping medical charts isn't a problem for you. No wonder you looked so amazed at our old-fashioned paper ones." She giggled a little. "Jed, even though we started to take notes by computer some time ago, they are still printed and bound into paper folders. If someone has a health problem it quickly begins to look like some medieval tome, and they are hard to keep track of and file." She sighed. "Not that it's a problem I'll have again, looks like."

"Sounds like that is a good thing."

A'lina finished and pointed the device at a projection screen that she had pulled out of the low ceiling. It registered a symbol for a moment, changing a little, the the symbol vanished and the muddled images of a human insides appeared on it. Jed realized the symbol had been the equivalent of a human computer 'loading, please wait', for now A'lina put the instrument back and stepped up to the screen with a pointer. Jed bit back a chuckle. He'd tell Gabi later about "Professor" A'lina, but now was not the time.

"I am fairly sure... " she began, "and please understand that I have never scanned a pregnancy in a human before, only read some of your books about it, but I would say that you are close to twelve weeks along."

She pointed at what to Jed's uneducated eyes looked amazingly like - a baby. He caught his breath, squeezing Gabi's hand in his own. He turned to look at her "You are amazing."

She giggled a little and turned shining eyes to him. "Why? why am I amazing?"

"Because you are carrying our child..."

"Actually, " A'lina interrupted. "Children."

They looked back up at the screen and saw what she was pointing to... another baby hovered at the other side of Gabi's uterus. They could see the faint line of the two amniotic sacs pressing together between them. "Wow," Jed breathed. "Twins."

Good News and Bad

Some time later Jed was back in the conference room with A'fri and J'red. He still felt stunned. He grinned at the two aliens and announced "I'm going to be a father."

They lit up and congratulated him, but the fire in their faces died so quickly that Jed knew something was wrong. He sobered and sat with them.

"So what is up, and is there anything I can do?"

A'fri shook his head. "No, I am afraid not. We are having to be very stealthy in our retreat from Earth. The Fleet Prince has many more ships covering the Earth than we had anticipated. Ordinarily there are only one or two clusters of ships, but here?" He gave that movement of shoulders and wings that Jed was learning was akin to a shrug, but much more complicated and meaningful. This one, he thought, meant 'life is never certain, and all gambles come to an end.'

"What are they usually watching for?"

"Anything that might threaten one of their ships. They will, by now, have taken out the computer systems controlling as much of the missile systems that they can find."

Jed shook his head. "Not Cheyenne Mountain or SAC in Nebraska... what's left of it, anyway."

"Oh, yes." J'red spoke for the first time, "those would have been the first they neutralized."

"How?"

"They have... hackers, you call them, and it is a good word for what they do. They have hackers that you would not believe. They have proven themselves over and over. The G'his regard them as the most powerful weapon in their arsenal."

"Our more immediate problem." A'fri overrode the brewing discussion firmly. "Is that we are going to be a few days reaching the carrier. We do not have the proper facilities for that length of time, so we need to be aware of that and prepare for it."

The discussion that followed helped assuage Jed's fears somewhat. With this, at least, he could be of use. He hated feeling useless. His whole adult life had been spent training and very little doing, but at least he knew that he could do what was asked. Hurtling through space trapped in a tin can with his pregnant wife and a bunch of aliens he hardly knew was not something he had trained for. Living on next to nothing... now that he could handle. So he was almost cheerful, and the Orioness regarded him with an emotion approaching awe, he noted.

That night he and Gabi slept in the reclining chairs in the sick bay. They had been offered the tiny cabin, but found the nests the Orioness preferred too strange to be comfortable. Jed held her hand all through the night, and lay awake for a long while staring at the faintly luminous ceiling and thinking about fatherhood. He was just thinking of the possibility of a son when he drifted off.

For the next two weeks, by Earth time, they did very little. Gabi and Jed did some gentle calisthenics together in the morning, trying to keep from getting too stiff, but with their heightened metabolisms, and the additional draw on Gabi's system, they dared not burn too many calories. Mostly, they and the crew talked. When the carrier finally loomed in the viewscreen, they were much more comfortable with one another.

There was quite a reception waiting for them as the gangplank lowered. Paul was right in front, with his arm over the shoulder of a short, roly poly woman with a fluff of silver hair. She smiled and waved as they stepped out, a little shaky at the renewed gravity. They had gotten used to the lower gravity in the smaller ship without even realizing it. Paul just beamed with pleasure.

Jed took his hand in silence and shook it. "Glad to see you made it."

"We managed to get out without the G'his coverage you had to deal with. We've been here almost two weeks already, waiting."

Gabi hugged Paul, and turned to the older woman. "You must be Margaret."

They looked at one another for a moment. Jed thought his wife had never looked more beautiful, dirty hair, smudged cheek and all. They had not had the water to wash with, and he knew they must smell pretty rank, but Paul's mother never hesitated as she pulled Gabi into her arms and declared "I am Maggy, and you must be exhausted, you poor lamb."

Gabi astonished him then by bursting into tears and clinging to Maggy's shoulder.

"Tsk. We are going to get you into a nice hot bath first thing, and then get a decent meal into you. Paul" She called over her shoulder as she led Gabi off. "See to Jedediah, won't you, dear?"

Jed turned back to Paul, his mouth hanging open slightly.

"Yep," Paul grinned "She has that effect on most people. Dad calls her a human whirlwind. He has trouble with his arthritis, so he doesn't get around much, or he would have come to meet you. We'll go see him later, but right now I'd better do as Mom says and get you fed and washed. Your troop wants to see you, too. They don't say it, but they have been pretty tense."

Jed blinked, digesting all this. "My troop? Oh. Well, usually they call a small group of soldiers a squad, and I don't know that they are mine..."

Aboard Ship and Underway

Gabi jumped and made a small squeak
as a soldier materialized at her shoulder
with a small rustle of fabric. She glared
at him. "Timmons, is it?"

"Yes'm" he grinned at her, his face
semi-obscured beneath a mask of chameleon
fabric. In the sterile corridors of the
ship, hiding places were few and far
between. The soldiers depended on shadows
and breaking up of their outline to
conceal them.

"I am aware," she continued frostily.
"That this game is going to go on for
some time longer. And further, I am also
aware that you all have a bet on for who
can surprise me every day."

She was pleased to see his eyes
widen. Evidently this was supposed to be
a secret. Ha! Point one for her.
"However, if you scare these babies out
of me some fine day, not only are you
going to have to catch them," The blood
drained out of the visible portion of his
face. Point two. "But then you are going
to have to explain it to Colonel
McGregor."

Point three and set to Gabrielle
McGregor.

"Y-yes." He saluted and started to back away.

She held out her hand. "Chip, please."

He jumped. "Oh, yes, Ma'am."

He turned over the small chip with the information on how he had sneaked up on her and her surprise. Then he backed into the shadows and disappeared. She continued to the sick bay, grinning like the Cheshire cat. She may have gotten caught, and would have to hear about it from Jed, but she had given as good as she got!

The game had been going on for a week, and was likely to last another week. Jed, after lengthy discussion with the Orioness, had settled on this as the best way to train his men - for they were his now. The small band of humans had been exiled from Earth, but not from their commitment to someday return and get the G'his kicked off. There had barely been time for an exchange of instructions, and Gabi didn't know all the details, but her husband was now acting as a Colonel, and the men that had been infected with the symbiote, and a few more volunteers, were all aboard the ship with him, under his command.

They, and their Orioness counterparts training with them, would lay in wait and surprise whomever they could. The microchip records of these ambushes were handed over to their luckless prey, and every evening there was a debriefing. Topics ranged from how best to turn an ambush back on itself, to staying aware and keeping one's mind on where one was walking - usually that last was directed at A'lina, who was the stereotypical absent-minded professor. Gabi wasn't sure of the real value of the training - it was unlikely that she would ever be involved in combat onboard ship, or off, for that matter - but it seemed to keep the young soldiers from getting bored and acting up.

She walked into the sick bay and greeted A'lina and Maggy with a cheerful "Good morning, Ladies! Ready to check up on the twins?"

While they checked her belly in their own ways, she told them about her encounter in the corridor.

"Hmph!" Maggy snorted, her hands warm on Gabi's belly. "As if I'd let a young ijit catch a baby!"

She completed her examination. "Well, one of these little angels is socked down in the birth canal so far I can't feel his head proper. Have you been having trouble sitting lately?"

"Yes," Gabi admitted. "It is really uncomfortable."

A'lina smiled gently at her. "I would venture a guess that they will be born soon."

She activated the projection and all three of them watched the two unborn infants in silence for a moment. At this stage there was so little room left in Gabi's womb that they were entertwined. As they watched, the child that would be second-born put his thumb in his mouth and started sucking. Maggy sighed. "I never thought all this technology we used back on earth was really necessary - too invasive, most of it. But this, A'lina, this is marvelous."

"Thank you Margaret. I did not invent this, though. I just use it - and so can you, you know."

"Yes. And it does make me feel better about taking care of our little village in a starship. But I do wish those we left behind could get this technology."

Gabi stayed reclining in the chair while they all talked about the few minor cases they had. There was one other woman who was now pregnant - one of Gabi's cousins, and Maggy was caring for her, as well. Gabi and A'lina took care of the few cases of injury. Most of them were the result of soldiers without the symbiote trying to compete with the enhanced men. The research into what exactly the symbiote did for all of them was still on-going, as well.

"Gabi, I still think that even given the presence of nannites, the symbiote is completely an organism instead of a machine. I was not on the development team, you understand. No-one is still alive who was, and the only way to figure out what they did is to go backward from what we have..."

"I know. And to do that, we have to get it to stay still long enough to study it."

The nannites had proven to be terribly difficult to study. They had found no way to 'kill' them, and when cultured, the little things hid. Inside cells, usually. Gabi sighed in frustration. When they had tried to study the nannites inside of her own body, the cell damage had made her mildly ill and brought the wrath of her husband sown on them. He had spoken to A'lina in his quiet way, and made it very clear that they were not to tamper with his wife and unborn children. He had offered his own body, but by then A'lina had decided that they were not going to get a glimpse of the nannites at work.

Gabi's train of thought was interrupted by a quiet knock at the door.

"Come" A'lina called out.

Paul put his face in the door hesitantly. He looked nervous about entering this conclave of females. Gabi reflected that he looked even younger than he had when they first met. He was learning a lot from Jed, but was spending most of his time as liaison between the civilian and military portions of their group. Jed had his hands full with his soldiers, even if there were only thirty of them, and Paul became his voice on other matters. Jed had the most experience and training in arranging civil affairs and in leadership, but Paul was doing quite well.

"I have a question..." he began, looking at his mother. "Um, Mom, it's rather - er, personal?"

Maggy laughed. "I have a pretty good idea, but I'll not embarrass you too much. I think I'll go see how the quilting bee is going."

They had not been able to gather much in the way of supplies, and had found themselves short of blankets. Fortunately, Gabi's aunt had a good stash of fabric, and several of the ladies were converting it into quilts - even a couple of baby-sized ones, Gabi suspected. She joined them once in a while, but was not patient with the tedious stitching required.

Paul gave her a sideways hug as she left and murmured "Thanks for understanding, Mom."

Gabi started to stand, rolling to one side off the chair, and Paul jumped to give her a hand. "Thank you."

Once standing, she looked at him and said "Ok, spill it."

A'lina, seated on a tall stool by the workbench, put down what she had been working on and looked him too.

He rubbed the back of his neck, looking abashed. "Oh, well, what I wanted to know is... if I am intimate with someone, how is the symbiote going to..." he waved a hand vaguely in the air."

"Ah. I had wondered when this was going to come up."

"Hmm," A'lina's contemplative sigh was more of a musical trill, but they were accustomed to it. "I do not know, but I suspect... nothing. As long as you do not actually secrete inside her, of course."

Paul looked briefly horrified. "Um, I meant I wanted to kiss her!"

"Oh."

Gabi couldn't last any longer, and burst out laughing. "I'm sorry," she finally gasped, "but the looks on your faces!"

Paul made a face at her. "I want to ask Tabby to, um, go steady with me."

"Tabby?" Gabi snorted. "Paul... oh, of course you're sure. It's just that I didn't think she was interested in boys yet. She still thinks of herself as a Valkyrie, you know. It was all Aunt Nia could do to persuade her to come and not stay and fight." she sighed. They would all have preferred to stay, but there was no choice. The Orioness had made it very clear what would happen to them if they stayed and the G'his found them.

"I know. And I know she has a lot of growing up to do still. But... she's special." A little smile quirked the side of his mouth as he looked off into space.

Gabi shook her head. "Just be careful with her heart, my friend. Her brothers will take you apart if she sheds so much as a tear."

"And there should be no problems if you choose to kiss her." A'lina assured him. "Although I would like to see the young lady and check her over, as I do not think I have met her yet. There is a slim chance that she will have a severe allergic reaction to the byproducts of the symbiote, and I would prefer to rule that out."

Paul paled slightly. "Yes, of course. I'm going to go find her now, if you will excuse me."

After he left Gabi looked seriously at A'lina. "You know, we are going to have to deal with a lot of this. And I am a little worried about the numbers."

"The numbers?"

"The fact that there are about a dozen unattached girls to more than twice that many boys. Oh, brother. What am I going to do?" she pantomimed pulling her hair out.

"Why is it your responsibility?"

"Because I seem to be the First Lady, that's why. I am married to Jed, who is ipso facto the leader of humanity off-planet, and that means I will be the one they come for a shoulder to cry on. Also, I seem to attract lovelorn youths. I was the unofficial counselor all through college and at the Institute."

"You will have your hands full with your children soon."

"True." Gabi felt a little better, and then realized something. "No, all that means is that I'll be tied down in one place and they can find me more easily. Argh!"

A'lina trilled a laugh at her friend's histrionics. "Perhaps you should speak to Nia and Maggy about this. They are the ones with the most maternal experience. And why shouldn't they be the ones these 'lovelorn youths' will speak to?"

"Because most of them are their children,and they aren't about to spill their guts to either their mother, or their intended's mother."

"True."

"But I am going to talk to them. I don't know why it took me so long to think of this. The pregnancy must be affecting my brain. Do you need me for anything?"

"No." A'lina shook her head, a human mannerism she had adopted. "Go ahead.

Please don't stay on your feet for too long. I want to keep your blood pressure down."

"All, right, mother."

"Oh, no," she heard as she stepped through the doorway. "That makes me grandmother to humanity, and I'm not that old!"

Gabi told Jed that night that neither of the community's matrons had been surprised at her questions. The three of them had taken tea together and had a good talk. He held up a hand at this, laughing "I'm not sure I want all the gory details, love."

She sniffed at him. She would have thrown a pillow, but they were all behind her back, supporting her bulk. Jed was sitting on the end of the bed, rubbing her feet. She wiggled her toes and smiled her appreciation as he continued rubbing.

"I hadn't thought of it either, tell you the truth. And you are right. The Bastita's and Halloran's are along together because the Colonel did think of that." Now he sighed. "Command is a lot harder than it looks from below."

"I'm sure it is, dear," she answered demurely.

He gave her a dirty look. "And as for you, since when did you become the model wife?"

"Since I didn't have anywhere else to run to," she admitted. "I have to say, I

kind of like it, really. You are...
impressive to watch. I've never gotten to
see you in action before, and I think
it's amazing that you never used any of
your persuasive skills on me."

His face softened and he crawled up
next to her to hold her in his arms. She
rested her head against his chest,
listening to his heartbeat. "I thought
about it," he rumbled into her ear. "But
I didn't want to keep you tied into
something you didn't want, weren't ready
for."

He kissed her hair gently. "I'm glad
you are happy, even with everything that
is happening."

She looked up at him. "Yes, I am.
When I stop to think about it I get
anxious, but most of the time I am too
busy. And the children help."

They started to move, on cue, and
they stopped talking for awhile to feel
the antics of their unborn children.

Sanctuary

Ten months after they left Earth, the forty-nine refugees crowded together in the observation deck to get a glimpse of the planet they were about to land on, and to discuss what was to become of them. Actually, there were fifty-one present, but the two littlest could not yet speak, and had never seen Earth.

Jed looked down at his wife, leaning back in a chair with her eyes closed and a child at her breast. One of the other women must have the other one. Gabi looked worn thin, but Maggy had assured him that this was a temporary thing, and his wife was dealing well with new motherhood and all the other stresses on her.

He stepped up onto a low table and began his little speech. "Friends and Family."

Everyone stopped talking and looked up at him. He continued "We will be landing within a couple of hours - not the Ch'liss itself, but shuttled to the surface. This is not the Orioness home planet, which is occupied by the G'his and has been badly damaged. But they have had a colony on this one for a couple of hundred years, so it will be pretty civilized. We will be here for quite a while. Their days are longer than ours - about 30 hours, by our reckoning - and that will take some getting used to. Their language is different. With a couple of exceptions, we aren't built to speak it, so we will have to wear translators at all times.

"I know it will be difficult, but all of you were selected because you have adventurous minds and that bullheaded quality that carries you through 'interesting times'"

In the back of the crowd, Lewis chuckled. Jed carried on, "We will be learning, mostly, getting up to speed on Galactic standards. We will be preparing along with the Orioness and a couple of other alien races you will be meeting, to carry the fight back to Earth and to boot the G'his out of our solar system!"

A ragged cheer went up at this. Most of them knew what would happen, had already made arrangements for living quarters, and some, like Gabi, already had appointments to the University. But Jed had wanted to spell things out and bond them together as a group one last time. It would be too easy to drift apart in the busy years to come without a strong bond. He hopped down off the table and kissed Gabi, who was smiling at him.

"Nice speech." she told him quietly.

"Thanks. Want to get a look at D'rass?"

"Yes, thank you." She took his arm. The symbiote had made her recovery from childbirth as easy as any Maggy had ever seen, but she was still awkward about getting up while supporting a nursing baby. He levered her off the lounge and regarded the calm face of his child with awe.

"Does he ever come off?"

"Yes. He's just got a lot of growing to do in a hurry. He wants to catch up with his daddy."

Jed laughed as they threaded through the clumps of people gathered by the screens. "Where is Bridget?"

"Karen has her. Did Juan talk to you yet?"

"No. What's up?

"Well, Karen and I decided that we re going to share households for awhile. She wants to stay home with little Domingo, and I want to go to school again right away."

"Oh..." Jed contemplated this for a moment. Juan and Karen Batista were the oldest of his soldiers. Karen was definitely due some time off - she had been days away from leaving the service when called to join her husband on this crazy adventure. She hadn't even batted an eye, just grabbed her ready bags and gone. Juan was the top sniper they could grab - a very good one - and that was a skill the Orioness said they could use, so that was why he had been asked to "volunteer".

Jed sighed. Juan was also the second-ranking soldier under his command - but he was not an officer. On the other hand, did it matter? His wife cut through his thoughts.

"We have located the Orioness version of a duplex, right on the University campus. So we wouldn't be sharing living quarters, just be close enough to help one another out."

"That sounds fine." He chuckled. "Although why you asked me I'm not quite sure."

She made a face at him, but then smiled. "I like to keep you briefed on these things."

"Yes, Mrs. Colonel."

She turned away from him and looked at the screens. The planet looming up in them was half in darkness, the visible half luminous and pearly. Mostly it was cloud cover, but she could see one part that was greenish blue. The swirls of clouds were visible from here, but then they could just make out a tiny speck that was a shuttle coming to get them.

Gabi tightened her grip on his arm. "I don't know why I am so nervous." she whispered, looking at it.

"It's one more step away from Earth." he replied, holding her. "But it is also one step closer to it." and he was glad she could not see his face, because he was looking forward to returning to Earth. The Orioness had briefed him on what had happened on their home world, and on the other worlds the G'his had touched, even in passing. He was afraid for Earth.

Cedar Sanderson is a writer, blogger, and businesswoman who can be found in her office pounding the keyboard when she isn't out walking the dog. Her work has been published by Stonycroft Publishing, Naked Reader Press, and Something Wicked. She is the author of the young adult novel Vulcan's Kittens, and her second novel, Pixie Noir, will be released late 2013. She writes regular blog columns at Amazing Stories Magazine and Mad Genius Club, in addition to her own writing blog, where she posts almost daily. She prefers science fiction, mostly writes fantasy, and dabbles in non-fiction when her passion is stirred.

Trickster Noir Teaser

Upcoming May 2014

I was dying, to begin with. Not in the long-drawn out way that everyone is, dying by days. No, I was going quickly. And my biggest regret was that I had never slept with Bella. Not in the way you are thinking, although I'd dreamed about that often enough. No, simply in the warmth of her arms with the peace of the night wrapped around us. I wondered if I would be aware in the afterlife, to regret this eternally.

I also regretted the burden I was about to drop on Devon's slim shoulders. He was a good lad, but still a lad, and nowhere near ready to be Duke. Maybe I ought to have just died quietly in her arms, rather than letting my dreams out of the box at this late date. I didn't want the Dukedom, I wanted her.

People came in and out of the room, but I don't remember who was there. Bella kept crying but not letting anyone see her. She thought I was out of it, and mostly I was, sometimes I was just too tired to look awake. It had been some time since I'd proposed, I wasn't sure how long. I wasn't staying awake long enough to know if it had been days, hours, or only minutes since I last opened my eyes.

My magic was gone. She'd stripped the elfshot, and with it had gone the magic. I tried for Sight, and got only the gray sparkles that happen if you squeeze your eyes shut for too long. So when Mark came and sat by my bed at some point, I was unable to confirm if he had magic, or I'd been mistaken back in Alaska.

"You didn't go home?" I asked, startling him. He had been nodding off and obviously not expecting the dead man to talk to him.

"Er," he rubbed his eyes and yawned. "Alger offered to teach me how to use magic. Seems I have some."

"So why are you sitting here?" I was genuinely curious. I'd barely met him, him sitting watch over me was hardly his debt to pay.

"Bella needed to sleep. Alger's sitting with her to make sure she does. Ellie's worn to the bone, and you mother was summoned to Court." His explanation was punctuated by a venture to the small table where a coffee urn stood. The smell wafting from his cup when he came back made my stomach growl, which startled both of us. I didn't remember the last time I'd eaten. I had vague memories involving a spoon, and something either warm or cool.

"Would you like some? Or can you have it?" He looked uncertainly down at me. Flat on my back, I couldn't drink it.

"Hell if I know." I admitted. I tried to sit up, the blankets an unendurable obstacle to that idea. He gently slipped an arm under my shoulders and I decided to let him. Once I was sitting, we found, I could stay up, wavering like a leaf in the wind. He grabbed cushions off the little couch and got me propped.

"Thanks."

"Don't mention it."

I was worried that I wouldn't be able to hold the cup, but that I could manage. I sipped slowly. It tasted wonderful with lots of cream and a little sugar.

"Ichor of the gods." I quipped with my old joke. He grinned suddenly, a flash of white teeth in dark brown beard.

"Longest I've seen you awake in a while." Mark was right, I realized. I didn't feel like I was going to fade out and fall over, either.

"I needed coffee." I reached up a hand to my own chin, letting the cup nestle in the coverlet folds to keep it secure. I was almost as bearded as he was. "By the Hunt! How long has it been?"

"Bella's the only one you will let near you, mostly. She was worried about trying to shave you with Alger's razor -

I think cutthroat was the word she used –
so it's been about six weeks. And man, it
ain't becoming."

"I don't have face foliage like you
do, no matter how long it's been," I shot
back at him. My beard was straggly, so I
was used to keeping my face smooth. I
fingered the hair again. "You know where
that razor went?"

A look crossed his face. "You kill
yourself with that blade, Bella will kill
me."

I snorted and leaned back against
the pillow. "I have safety razors. Alger
obviously didn't look in the cupboard."

I told him where he'd find them,
and as he walked across the room, closed
my eyes to rest the eyelids. They were
heavy after so long not being awake, it
turned out. I woke up again to daylight,
and no Mark. But... I managed to touch my
chin. I was lying flat again, but my arms
were above the coverlet so I could move.
I was smooth shaven. Good man.

"You're awake." And that was
mother's voice, sounding rather pleased.
I turned my head.

"How long?" I croaked. She
fluttered a bit, finally coming up with a
glass of water and a straw. I sipped
gratefully.

"Since?" She was trying to deflect,
not a good sign.

I sighed. "Since I talked to Mark?"

She relaxed. "That was yesterday. Or last night, rather."

"Bella?"

"She'll be up shortly, she's having lunch with Ellie in the kitchen. I took over for an hour, firm. Poor girl needs to rest, too."

"She does. And doesn't need to be tied to my wrecked old hulk."

She blinked in surprise. I suppose I sounded morose. I growled a little under my breath. I just wanted to die in peace, was that too much to ask?

"Are you hungry?" she asked.

"Do I get to sit up if I am?"

She sighed. "Let me go get Mark."

She was almost out the door before I could respond, calling after her, "He's not my valet!" I finished in my head, having run out of breath, I don't have a valet, I don't need a valet, I'm not some old doddering fool or a Court dandy.

I lay there, panting slightly from that exertion. I could hear murmurs in the hall, but not what was being said. I wondered if Alger would give me grace. This was impossible. I would not be a burden for what remained of my worthless life. I rolled over, feeling like even that was a monumental accomplishment, and a wave of weakness washed over me. I wasn't going to be able to stand up, much less make it to the bathroom. I didn't want to think about those provisions for the weeks previous.

The coverlet was the next obstacle. I'd never realized before just how heavy the damn thing was. No-one was walking through the door just yet. In that moment of aloneness I realized just how oppressive it had been to never be alone, even if I had been unconscious. I wanted my armory. The legs over the edge of the bed was a bad idea, in retrospect. They were heavy as lead, and about as easy to move.

Actually, once they had momentum, they worked just fine. As anchors. I slid out of the bed and landed on the floor with a jarring thud.

That worked. Time to start crawling, probably better than trying to walk just now. The nightshirt was tangled around my legs and not helping. I honestly wasn't sure if I was looking for a weapon to kill myself with, or just get to the bathroom. Footsteps sounded, coming through the door.

I looked up at Bella. She crouched down next to me. "Where are you going?" She had a funny look on her face.

"Bathroom," I gasped out. She nodded. Mark appeared on my other side, and together they got me to my feet. I refuse to admit that I whimpered when I took that first step.

"Bella!" My mother, sounding both scandalized and afraid.

"Lucia, he needs to move. If he stays in bed he's going to die. Or waste away to nothing. If he's out of bed, he's ready to walk."

Mother Titania, I loved this woman. Dying was worth having the right to call her mine. They got me in the bathroom, and I promised I would rap on the door when done. That business over with, I didn't want to go back to bed. Mark half-carried me to the little couch, while mother and Bella had a low-voiced but very tense discussion over my husk. I was beginning to feel like laughing when Ellie appeared with a tray of sandwiches, and my stomach made a rude noise again. She looked pleased to see me sitting up, at least. For once I didn't mind all the people in my room. As long as I was awake and alive to see them.

Food was both delicious, and exhausting. People were less and less welcome as I tired again. But I had been up for a whole hour, easily the most since... Well, I don't want to think about that.

"Bella..." I was now surrounded by what seemed like most of my family. I wasn't sure she could hear me over the talking, and I didn't have the strength to project. She stood up.

"Everyone out. Yes, he's better. But mostly he needs rest."

She'd read my mind. I leaned back, watching as she efficiently herded them out, gentle and inexorable.

"I'm not ready to get back in the bed." I told her after the last of them had the door closed behind them.

"Ok. When you fall asleep I'll go get Mark, though."

"I have questions," I started. She came to sit next to me, easy in her soft blue dress. I wondered about her jeans, and then realized that they wouldn't be available Underhill. Bringing my wandering mind back to my point, "No one is using magic around me. On purpose, or?"

She nodded. "When the smallest spell is activated in your room, you... twitch. It was decided," which most likely meant she had put her foot down, hard, "that we would not use it around you. I wanted to take you home, honestly, but they wouldn't allow it, and I wasn't sure what to tell a doctor was wrong with you."

Massive internal bleeding, broken bones, and complications from a mind rape. I felt my face flinch. She put a hand on my cheek. "I was sure I was going to lose you."

"You still might. Bella, I..." I swallowed hard. "I don't think I'm going to make it. I've been ill before, with the elfshot. This is, different. I can't even access the Sight. There's nothing."

She shook her head, smiling a little. "You had me worried up until last night. Wanting to shave was a sure sign that you were coming back from the edge."

"I lost my magic."

She shrugged. "There's a whole world of people without it up above. You're alive, and you have been doing very little with magic for a long time, I talked to Alger about it."

I sighed. I couldn't explain what I was thinking, that if I had to be helpless, dependent on others for everything, I didn't want to be alive.

"Will you sleep with me tonight?" Now I did succeed in startling her.

"I don't know..." she began dubiously, and I could tell she was trying to figure out how to say this.

"Just sleep."

"I've been sleeping here," she patted the couch cushions. "But yes, I would like that."

She put her head on my shoulder, not resting any weight on me, and I realized I was all skin and bones. No wonder I was having trouble moving, my muscles were shot. If I wasn't going to die, that was going to have to change.

I fell asleep like that, her warm against my side. I woke up to her curled up under the covers with me. Someone, likely Mark and Bella, had tucked me into bed. It was what I had wanted, but I lay there staring at the ceiling, worrying. What if something did happen to me, despite her assurance that I would be recovering now? I needed to talk to Alger, who seemed to be avoiding me. He had been part of the hubbub earlier, but hadn't talked to me, and I hadn't noticed until later.

Bella rolled over. "Hey."

Her eyes were only half-open and her hair tangled over her face. She pushed it back, and I could see her face pale in the half-light of the room. "I didn't mean to wake you."

"I'm not used to sleeping with someone. And I have been a bit worried about you. I was..." she paused, and in the dark I couldn't see her expression, but I could hear the tears when she went on "You got really still."

"I'm still here."

"I almost didn't sleep with you tonight. I was afraid I'd hurt you."

I huffed a short laugh. "Roll over on me and smother me? You're not that big, Bella."

She sniffed. "All right, it wasn't rational. But this wasn't how I wanted our first night to go."

"Me, neither." I reached out and took her hand. I wanted to hold her, but she was right, it would hurt.

[ ]

Bella woke up with a start. There was another person in bed with her... she was in a bed, first time in weeks. Lom! She rolled over carefully. He was breathing softly, still alive. She relaxed and watched him sleep. It was full daylight, and although the curtains were drawn, she had enough light to really study him.

His face was thin and pale. Asleep, she couldn't see the pain lines around his eyes, but the deep crushed-violet circles under them were not reassuring. She didn't know what had happened under Baelfire Tower, not all of it. His injuries from the physical side were healed, thanks to Melcar on the spot to take care of the immediate trauma, and the time since, but she was very afraid that her using the poison of the elfshot had been what was keeping him from fully healing.

She slipped out of bed without waking him and went to the room across the hall. When it had become obvious that he wasn't recovering anytime soon, Ellie had asked if she would like this room. It was closed, dusty, and very empty, had been for a long time. Bella knew very well that there was history in this house she knew nothing about. Ellie, who had hired or just called in a favor, Bella wasn't sure which, had brought in a crew of wood elves to help around the house. Alger, Lucia, Devon, and Mark were all staying here, in rooms that stretched improbably off the end of a hall she knew had not been there before. Fairyland was strange, and it hurt her brain if she thought too hard about it.

She had a bed, and clothes in the wardrobe, but not much else, and it didn't feel like home. Bella looked around the room. The brocade wallpaper was gaudy and hideous. Dressing took only a moment, and pulling a brush through her hair to re-braid it not much longer. She kept thinking she was going to cut it short, but there was no time. Ready for the daytime, she slipped back into Lom's room.

He was still sleeping soundly, she saw. This seemed to be a natural sleep, though, not the coma he had been slipping in and out of for so long. Bella bent over him and could see the movement of eyes beneath his closed eyelids. He dreamed. This was a good thing. She resisted the urge to kiss him, lest she wake him up, and retreated to the couch, where there was less temptation, and a book on the table.

Carrying a library in her head was, she had decided months ago, a wonderful thing. But paper was still nice, too. She had this, Thaumaturgy for Wylde Beastes, in her head, but it helped her organize her thoughts to look at it in paper. For one thing, what she was thinking of as the search engine in her brain, was not terribly controlled and from time to time she would be overwhelmed in answers when asking a simple question. Besides, the old books smelled good.

The house was still and silent, and Bella wondered what time it was. Time Underhill was not linear. She had never seen the moon, here, and although a sun rose and set, the night skies were milky, with a pearly opalescence. No stars, which she missed. She wondered what season it was back at her cabin, and had anyone remembered to clean out the refrigerator?

Ellie put her head in the door and looked at Bella. Bella nodded silently and came out into the hall, relieved at the interruption, as she wasn't focusing well on her studies.

"How is he?" Ellie asked.

"He seems to be dreaming. He's..." Bella looked for the right words to describe how she felt. "He's there, again."

Ellie nodded, smiling. "There will be breakfast and coffee shortly, then. But this came, and I thought you needed to see it right away."

She handed over a small, stiff envelope sealed with red wax. Bella was reminded again just how archaic some customs in this place were. She'd seen the seal before, on notes that came requesting a status update every few days. This missive from the king, she was sure, was not another of those.

She opened it slowly, apprehensive. This whole business of having a king still rubbed her wrong, and he hadn't been the most rational person in their dealings.

Consort-Elect Belladonna,

We summon thee to an audience with the King and Council on this day. An escort to Court will be provided.

The signature was scrawled so she couldn't read it. Short, to the point, and left her feeling like she hadn't a clue. Bella handed the note to Ellie.

"What does it mean?"

Ellie's face betrayed her surprise at being shown the royal summons. She was Lom's most trusted retainer, Bella knew, and Bella also knew she was intelligent and had a mind of her own, she wasn't simply a servant.

"I don't know enough about Underhill to not put my foot in my mouth," Bella explained, "I am going to need help if I'm going to protect his good name."

"I don't know what it is about.
Lucia may, she has been at court
recently."

Which was also Ellie's delicate way
of referring to Lucia's ability to keep
her ear to the ground when it came to
Court gossip. Bella had no doubt that
between Margot and Lucia, the King had an
efficient internal intelligence
operation, had he the sense to use it.

Bella looked toward Lom's room.
They had all been rotating through
sitting with him, never leaving him
alone. Ellie shooed her down the hall.
"I'll stay, you get breakfast. Lucia is
in the great room."

Bella nodded her thanks and went.
Coffee was sounding better and better, as
she had slept deeply last night, leaving
her groggy. Note in hand, she collected a
mug of coffee from the kitchen before
finding Lucia seated at a desk under one
of the tall, mullioned windows. Lom had
indulged himself with this place, Bella
thought again.

"Lucia?"

The older pixie looked up sharply,
her crisply arranged white hair framing
her pale face perfectly. Bella had never
seen her anything other than immaculately
made up, which kept her from looking
washed out. Lucia was the epitome of old-
fashioned grand-dame.

"Good morning, Bella. Is he...?"

One thing about her future mother-in-law, she truly did love her son. "He's sleeping, and dreaming. I wanted to ask your advice."

Bella handed the older woman her note. Lucia pulled a set of half-moon framed glasses out of somewhere and slipped them on before reading.

"Ah, I wondered how long he would wait," she commented after a quick perusal.

"Do you know what this is about?"

"You are to be his consort, and there are many things you do not know yet."

Bella felt a wave of frustration pass over her, but she tried not to show it. "I'm well aware that I am ignorant, and frankly, don't want to be his consort."

That, and it just felt wrong to be called a consort. She knew it was supposed to be a strictly political position, but she was a one-man woman. Bella glanced upward, wishing he were awake. His cool, calm insight was what she needed.

"My dear," Lucia held out her hands. Bella allowed her to take one of hers into her grasp. "I know this must be terribly confusing, as you were not brought up here. But you must understand this position is both a deep compliment to you, and the only way you can have the freedom to return home even if only for visits."

"What?"

"You are enormously powerful in magic. The likes of which has not been seen in many generations. Do you think the King would allow that kind of risk to be untrained in the world above? Only by accepting the consortship could you be trusted."

"Oh." Bella hadn't thought about this. That was Lom's job, to bring magically dangerous beings Underhill, to... what? She didn't know. Prison?

"What happens... is there a jail, or?" she groped for the concepts behind what she was thinking.

Lucia looked surprised. "I thought you knew."

Bella shook her head, feeling Lucia's fingers tighten on her own. "They are sent to the Wild Hunt, to be bound to the Huntsman. If they try to escape, they are hunted."

"That's what the Huntsman wanted of Lom."

Lucia nodded. Bella went on, feeling numb. "They would have sent me to the Hunt? And Lom..."

"Would never have allowed that to happen."

"I realize that. I didn't understand..." She pulled free of Lucia's hands and sat heavily in the nearest chair.

"When the Hunt came for him, Alger almost let them have him. I didn't understand - I still don't, and I wasn't about to let them anywhere near Lom in that condition. But what has he done, to be turned over to them?"

"I don't know. As a young man, I..." Lucia looked away, and Bella understood this to be hiding some great emotion. "I sent him away. To Alger, to be trained, but really he could have stayed at home. I don't know what happened, but the next time I saw him he was very ill," she imitated Bella's gesture and looked upward, "dying, really, and I made the second fatal mistake. He never trusted me again. It's been years, and his chosen profession has not made him friends, Underhill, despite it being for their own good."

"I think I understand. Cops, up in my world, aren't always liked, either."

"He's not..." Lucia fluttered a little, something Bella had never seen her do. "He's a bounty hunter, not respectable. It would be better..."

Bella interrupted her. "I know he hunts the monsters. I wanted to help him."

Lucia looked shocked, her smooth mask crumbling for an instant. "You are... you can't..."

"Why not?" Bella put her chin up a little. "Someone has to help him, and right now," they both looked up, "he's helpless." She finished softly. "So, tell me what I ought to wear to this audience, and I will go do what I must."

Dressed simply, but formally, she waited for her escort. Going to court under guard, especially knowing what her fate would be if she disobeyed the King's orders, was not helping her keep her calm. But for him, she must be compliant to her new role. At least she had been granted a reprieve while Lom was on the borders of death.

She didn't know either of the men who came for her, fairies in the familiar green and gold dress uniform of the court. They did not speak, and neither did she, simply stepping into the bubble and whisking off to the Kings antechamber.

Bella felt very alone. She was used to being alone, out in the wilderness, no people for miles. That felt safe, comfortable - that was home. Here, she was on edge, unsure of what was wanted from her, and with people who relied on her to get it right. Joe's wink, almost imperceptible, helped enormously as the double doors swung open, and she marched through with her head held high and an exterior calm.

The men and women of the council were seated around the vast rectangle of tables, the center of it left open for the speaker of the moment to pace and be able to be heard easily. The king slouched in his big chair on the dais, Bella didn't think the leather cushions and simple wood frame qualified it as a throne, but it suited him. She liked King Trytion despite herself. He was an even-handed ruler, from what she had seen. There was an empty chair, and she went to it without pausing to ask directions. They had all been there a while, she could tell, from the cups and small plates in varying disarray on the table, and papers simply everywhere.

She nodded to the King before sitting, and he nodded back. The rest of the Council had fallen silent, and Bella could feel her palms start to sweat. She folded her hands in front of her.

"M'Lady Bella, Consort-elect, how is Duke Mulvaney?" The King spoke to her without much preamble, as she was learning was his way. This was not a flowery man, but very formal.

"My King, I believe he has finally begun to recover."

He smiled slightly, almost hidden beneath his beard and mustache. "This assures us that our decision to call you was correct."

Bella took a deep breath. She still didn't know enough protocol to know what she was about to mess up. "And, my lord, what did you call on me about?"

He sat up straighter and leaned forward. Across the table from her someone coughed, a man from the deep sound, but she refused to look away from the King, who was also ignoring the person trying to get his attention.

"A situation has arisen, one that we are accustomed to calling on Duke Mulvaney's services for. Unfortunately, as he is indisposed, we were hoping that you would be able to step into his role."

Bella tried not to let her jaw drop open. "You want... me? To go after a monster?"

"It was made clear to us that he considers you a partner. As such, and without other alternatives..." So that was what they had all been discussing so fervently before her arrival. Looking for someone, something else, to rid them of this problem. She lifted her chin a little.

"I am willing." Her voice rang out, far clearer and firmer than she thought possible. "What is it, that makes you willing to risk losing me?"

He nodded slightly. "That is a grave risk. Yet this is also a grave danger to Our Kingdom, and you would be a rare Queen-consort with your power. We cannot wrap you up in wool and keep you hidden in Court. Nor would we send you out on a suicide mission, nor alone."

His eyes softened a little. She knew he would like to say more, but not in a room full of hostile ears. "There is a briefing packet for you, but in short, the nest of ogres you encountered once before has, due to the irritation of that fight, perhaps, become a visible nuisance."

"Ah." Bella leaned back in her chair and remembered that particular fight. Lom seemed to think the only one of them killed was the one she had blown apart with an incendiary rocket blast to the chest. Messy, scary, and they had been working as a team. Lom had gone bowling for ogres with a logging truck, for goodness sakes, and now she was supposed to take on a whole nest by herself?

"And I may put together a team?" She asked quietly, still not looking at anyone but him. This time, the man across the table did speak up. She could see on the faces of those surrounding him that they were in agreement, but he was their appointed spokesman.

"Consort-elect..."

Bella interrupted him, knowing she was being terribly rude, "and you are?"

He ignored her and went on, "one of the great benefits of Lom was that he

always worked alone. So there was less...
disturbance, above."

Bella filled in mentally, 'and so
if he died, there would be fewer
witnesses.'

He rumbled on, lacing his hands
together in front of him on the table and
looking down his nose at her. "He fit in
above, at least somewhat, which few of
our people have the training to do. You,
for obvious reasons, will do so as well.
We are unwilling to risk further exposure
in this matter, bad enough already as it
is."

She blinked at him. So, not a
suicide mission, eh? Something came to
her mind, and she looked back at the
king, who had gone all stone-faced again.
"My cousin, Mark, who remained Underhill,
could assist me."

The king shook his head, "Alger and
Mark were dispatched to an incident
Underhill about six hours ago. Discretion
is of the highest importance, and they
cannot be recalled."

Bella took a deep breath. "Then, by
your leave, I would take the packet and
go to gather tools for my assignment."
She swiveled her head back and glared at
the old fairy who had been her
opposition. "I do not know your name,
sir, but I trust that I am able to arm
myself?"